AMY REDEK

OUT IN THE
REAL
WORLD

GAY TRANSVESTITE EROTICA

WARNING

This book contains sexually explicit scenes and adult language. It may be considered offensive to some readers. This book is for sale to adults ONLY.

Please store your files wisely where they cannot be accessed by underage readers.

About the Publisher

4Fun Publishing, a member of **BLVNP Incorporated**, 340 S. Lemon #6200, Walnut CA 91789, info@blvnp.com / legal@blvnp.com
NOTE: Due to the highly emotional reaction of some people to works of erotic fiction, any email sent to the above address that contains foul language or religious references is automatically deleted by our anti-spam software and will not be seen. All other communications are welcome.

DISCLAIMER

Please don't be stupid and kill yourself. This book is a work of FICTION. Do not try any new sexual practice that you find in this book. It is fiction and not to be confused with reality. Neither the author nor the publisher or its associates assume any responsibility for any loss, injury, death or legal consequences resulting from acting on the contents in this book. Every character in this book is over 18 years of age. The author's opinions are not to be construed as the opinions of the publisher. The material in this book is for entertainment purposes ONLY. Enjoy.

Out In The Real World
Gay Transvestite Erotica

By: Amy Redek

© **Amy Redek 2015**
ISBN: 978-1-62761-813-7

'Why were you dressed as a woman when you were arrested?' the solicitor who had been assigned to me asked.

'I was on my way to work and stopped in the pub for a drink,' I replied.

'Work? Dressed as a woman? Why?'

That same old question, why. It cropped up many times before and yet there were still very few times that I could answer it. I gave out a sigh.

'I work in a transvestite night club as a female impersonator. Does that answer your question?' I asked.

'Not really. I would have thought that you would have been dressed in, ah, trousers and the like and changed when you got to work,' he said.

'I haven't any, ah, trousers and the like,' I said sarcastically. 'All of my wardrobe consists of women's clothes.'

'Why?'

'Oh for Christ's sake! Because I like dressing up as a woman!'

'Mr. Trent, or can I call you Jack?' he asked.

'Jackie. Everybody who knows me calls me by that name. I'm even billed under the name.'

'Okay. Jackie. I've been assigned by the court to defend you and so I must know something of your background and exactly what happened in that pub. The charge is affray, assault, damage to property, assaulting two police officers and resisting arrest as well as abusive language. How will you plead?'

'Not guilty, of course! I was only defending myself. She started it!' I said.

'But you put her into hospital as well as one of the police officers,' he said.

'Serves them both right. Her for starting it and him for grabbing me like he did, look!' I pulled up the torn sleeve of my dress and showed him the purple bruise marks on my upper arm, the imprints of fingers clearly to be seen. 'He shouldn't have gripped me so hard. I didn't know it was a copper when I swung round and hit him. I was only defending myself.'

'The other woman suffered a broken nose and cuts to her face from the glass you smashed into her face.' I gave a snort at this.

'Other woman my arse! That was Maurice Goodchild, also known as Maureen. A blowsy queen that shouldn't be out on the streets at her age.'

'Maurice Goodchild?' he asked, looking quite surprised at this news.

'Yes. I didn't know it was her tom I was chatting up while she was out in the cottages,' I said.

'Cottages?' he queried.

'Toilets to you,' I replied. 'He was sitting by himself and I thought he was good looking enough to have a chat with and so I sat down to talk. Next minute I was hit on the shoulder by Maureen who started screaming at me and she went and tore my sleeve so I hit her with my beer glass. I didn't know I had it in my hand, I thought I was using my fist. I know the glass broke in my hand and I could see blood coming from her nose but I wasn't going to give her a chance of hitting me back so I jumped on her.'

'Smashing two tables and a chair in the process,' my solicitor said.

'It was as much her fault as mine as well as her tom for he jumped on my back. It was him that caused us to crash into the other tables.'

'What's Tom's last name?' he asked. 'We may have to call him as a witness.'

'Tom?' I snorted. 'That's not his name! That's the name given to a man that picks up the likes of her. What his real name is I've no idea, I've never seen the man before.'

'Okay,' he said. 'So you started to chat him up, why?'

'Well if he was agreeable, we would have gone out to the cottages,' I said.

'Why?'

'What planet are you on? To have him fuck me, of course.'

'Oh! You mean you were actually soliciting then?'

'Am I being charged with that too?' I asked.

'No.'

'Then yes, I was. Isn't that what you do being a solicitor? Getting clients so that you can fuck them?' I asked with a smile.

'Not quite,' he said, having to laugh at the suggestion which made him almost human. 'That has already happened to them and we try to help them as best we can, like you.'

'I never got round to being fucked before the fight started,' I said.

'But you're fucked now unless I can get you off.'

***

As he said, he didn't get me off and so I was fucked. I was found guilty and sentenced to three months' prison. I don't suppose my turning up in court wearing a dress helped my case, but I was going to either win or go down with my colours nailed to the mast. My solicitor did the best he could but it was my kicking the second copper in the balls as I was being held that turned things against me.

I got a lot of sneers from the guards as I was dumped in Wandsworth Prison later that day. I won't go into all the names I was called by the guards in there as I had to strip off my clothes for a shower before being given my prison clothes to wear. I was escorted into C Block and up on the second tier, a cell door was opened and I was told to go in.

'Well bless me if it isn't Jackie Trent,' the lag on the upper bunk said as I went inside and heard the cell door clang behind me.

'Hallo Bert,' I said. 'Never thought that I'd meet you in here?' Bert Wilson was a pickpocket, though I think he was beginning to suffer from arthritis for he seemed to get caught more often now he was getting older. I knew him from the outside and he'd been into my club a few times.

'Why are you here?' he asked, sitting up and letting his legs dangle down.

'You know Maureen Goodchild?' I asked and he nodded. 'Well I gave her a new nose job and ruined a copper's love life, putting them both in hospital. They gave me three months.'

'Well this is going to upset your love life too then,' he chuckled.

'Not really for this is a men's prison and there must be quite a few who are quite randy. As I'm in here with you Bert, would you like to be the first?'

'I've got no money, Jackie,' he said a little disconcertedly.

'As we're going to be cell mates, it's free for you,' I said and saw his face light up in a smile which broadened even more as I stroked the front of his trousers and felt that he'd suddenly risen up.

'Oh Jackie,' he said as he slid off the top bunk and landed down next to me. 'Can I kiss you too?'

'Of course,' I said with a laugh as I undid my trouser buttons.

He grabbed me with his arms and gave me a good smacking kiss on the lips as I dropped my trousers and turned round and leaned down onto the lower bunk. Like me, he didn't give a hoot as to what the other cells on the other side of the block could see as I heard his trousers come down and felt the tip of his of erection press against my rear.

'Push in and fuck me, Bert. It's been two weeks since my last cock.'

I gave out a big sigh as I felt him push and enter my backside. It was lovely to have a cock back inside me again and I reveled in his movements as he shafted me, almost drooling as he held my hips firm as he fucked me. I think he might have been without anything like this for a long time for he was soon holding me tight as he came, bucking his hips. I felt his seed spatter my insides and welcomed the soothing massage he was giving me.

It was over too soon and I gave out a mew as he pulled out and staggered to the metal basin to wash his cock before putting it away. I'd pulled my trousers up and got onto the lower bunk and sighed at just having had a lovely fuck. When he'd finished, he turned and got onto the bunk with me and gave me a kiss.

'Thanks Jackie, you don't know how much I needed that,' he said as he kissed me again.

'Anytime, Bert, anytime. I'm not going anywhere for the next three months,' I said, reliving the pleasure of having a hard penis rouse my insides again. 'Who's the Baron?' I asked, that being the term for the prisoner who was the top dog of the place.

'Eddie Forbes,' he replied.

Bert didn't have to enlarge on that for I knew who Eddie Forbes was. He was a bank robber and was serving twelve years of which he'd already served four. I knew him by sight though not to talk to and I looked out for him when we went down to the mess hall for dinner. I queued up with the others for our supper and some was dumped on my metal tray and then looked for where this Eddie Forbes was sitting. I saw his table and walked over with my tray and though the table was full, I stopped by him.

'Can I sit down here?' I asked. There were some scowls from the others seated but not from Eddie. He looked me up and down and at least it was with frankness and not as if he was looking at a heap of shit.

'Certainly Jackie,' he said. 'Shift!' he demanded of the men that were sitting opposite him and so they started to shuffle their backsides along the bench and the guy at the end had to get up and with a scowl at me, moved onto another table as room was made for me opposite Eddie.

'So what does our catamite Jackie want of me?' he queried as I sat opposite him and began to eat from my tray. I smiled at him.

'Your cock and protection in either order,' I said, looking him in the eye. 'I'm willing to look after you if you'll look after me. There's too many pederasts in this place for my liking. I'd rather have you than any number of the others.'

'As I understand you've already had Bert Wilson,' he said with a smile.

'He's my cell mate. He was hospitable in his welcome to his humble abode and I returned that hospitality by welcoming him into mine.' He laughed at this as he continued his meal and looked at me with a speculative eye.

'So you are offering yourself to me in return for protection?'

'Unreservedly except for letting Bert ease himself now and again,' I said with a smile. 'Other than him, I will be yours to command, plus that I sit here opposite you for all my meals during my three months here.'

I wondered if I'd gone too far for he didn't answer me for several minutes as he continued eating his meal. In fact he didn't say anything till he'd finished eating and pushed his empty tray along to the man sitting next to him.

'Be in my cell in half an hour,' he said as he got up, leaving his tray for this other man to take away for him.

Got you, I said to myself. I knew that I was now safe from rape whilst inside for it was better to choose the man who was going to fuck you than have half a dozen or more suddenly attack you and force themselves inside and possibly cause some internal problems.

I finished my meal and after putting my empty tray with the others, left the dining hall and went up to my cell and stripped off and washed myself at the basin as Bert came in.

'So you're going with Eddie Forbes then,' he said in a flat voice to me.

'Yes Bert,' I said as I dried myself, 'but I made it quite clear that though I'm going under his protection, you will still be able to have me when we're alone in this cell.' That made his face light up having thought that with me now being Eddie's piece of meat, he wouldn't get a sniff or taste. 'See you before lights out,' I said as I left the cell and went along to that of Eddie's. One of his other minions was inside with him when I walked in.

'Fuck off,' he said to his cell mate, 'and just keep watch.' The other man got up without a word and left the two of us alone. I moved into Eddie and ran my hand inside his shirt.

'How do you want me?' I asked. 'Mouth or rear?'

'Let's see how good you are in giving head,' he said as he got onto the lower bunk and laid himself out. I went down onto my knees and undid his flies and pulled out his throbbing erection and held it upright in my hand. It was good to hold such a weapon again and look at, already starting to drool for I had been told that I was quite good in giving head. His was no bigger than most men and it was great to hold the hardness of a throbbing cock and feel his pulse rate through the fine skin that sheathed this muscle.

I gave it a few rubs first, feeling the strength of it before opening my mouth and lowering my head to take him inside. He was hot and my own cock rose up as I ran my tongue round the half-exposed head from its foreskin and gave out a big sigh through my nose as I began to suck on him as I worked his shaft with my hand. I was also able to get my erection out of my own hated trousers as I worked on his and jerked myself off as I strove to give him complete satisfaction in this way.

He gave out a grunt and began to buck his hips slightly as he began to come and come he did in quite a quantity that I took into my mouth as I came myself, shooting my load under the bunk as my mouth filled with his sperm. I held it there till he'd finished before swallowing the lot and carried on moving my hand as I squeezed the last drops out of the eye that I licked off.

'That was very good Jackie,' he said as I got his deflating prick back into his trousers before putting mine away. 'Tomorrow you'll work down in the laundry with me,' he said and then he got up from the bunk and gave me a kiss on the cheek. 'Down there we'll have the other end,' he said with a smile and pushed me out of his cell and beckoned in the other man.

I went off back to my own cell and Bert wanted to know all the details as our door closed along with the others'. I not only told him what I did, but showed him too. He was over the moon.

Next day after breakfast, I was taken to the laundry by a guard and handed over to the warder in charge there. He just told me to see Eddie as to what my duties would be, which turned out to be quite light. It wasn't long before he got me into a corner and told me to drop my trousers. This I did and then leaned over a basket trolley of washing and had the thrill of being fucked up the arse again. I needed it and would have taken more if he'd offered me to his mates, but he didn't.

So for those three months he either fucked me or I sucked on his cock. Not always in the same order, but at least twice a day he had me. Bert didn't go without either. There was the odd man I was given to by Eddie as part of a favour to which I had no objections for any cock that was up and rampant was acceptable to me to please me as well as the giver.

***

I was nearly in tears on my last day there as I was fucked by Eddie who, because of who he was, had kept other predators away from me. He'd stroked my bare bum and told me that he was going to miss having me as he stuck his prick in between the cheeks and gave me a good rogering. This was straight after breakfast for half an hour later, I was taken through to where I was given back my own clothes, the warder handing them to me with a look of distaste on his face at having to handle these women's things.

How nice it was to finally get rid of those hateful trousers and pull on a pair of stockings once again. The wearing of these soft clothes was what I had missed most these past three months, well, except for my gin and tonics too. I was left in a small room on my own to get dressed and being as perverse as I normally am, roused myself up to an erection and jerked myself off into my panties and left them inside the trousers for one of the warders to find later. Of the small amount of money I had been given for working in the laundry, I gave most to Bert, saving just enough for myself to get a taxi to the bank. Fortunately, the landlord where I lived was good and knew that I would pay my back rent when released.

This I did and I also got a right bollocking from the club manager when I turned up to see if I still had a job.

'Why the hell did you have to pick that night to have a fight and get arrested. A full club and our supposed star doesn't show up. Why?' he screamed at me.

There was that word being thrown at me again. Why! Why was I always being asked this? See, they've even got me using that bloody word. How the hell can you really explain what you'll ever do in every situation that you encounter? You can't. Anyway, even though I wanted to scream this back to him, I didn't for I still needed the work and so I mumbled out an apology and bit my tongue in case I said something that I would later regret.

It seemed to pay off for when he ran out of breath and words to describe my behaviour, he said that I could start that evening but I had lost top billing and I would have to do better than his new star to take back the top spot. Mind you, it wasn't the money that he paid that kept us all there, it was what we made out in the cottages, which was more than double what he paid us. I suppose that's why he never said anything about us using his club as an unofficial male brothel for we were, if the truth be really known and acknowledged, whores, selling our mouths and ring pieces to whoever had the money to fuck us in either orifice.

Mind you, I didn't do myself any favours that evening when I went into the dressing room.

'Jackie!' was screamed out as I entered the cramped dressing room by Sally. We always used our female names both in and out of the club. She was a few months younger than me and not as good looking as myself or sung any better. She was up from her seat, second from the end, and hurled herself at me, smearing her make-up as she kissed me. 'We thought you'd gone forever!' she cried as she embraced me. 'You'll have to tell us all about it. Shift you lot,' she cried out to the others. 'Move down and let Jackie have her place.' There were disgruntled noises from the other four as Sally began pushing them back towards the entrance. The end seat was always for the newcomer because you got knocked about every time one of the others went out or came into our confined space.

Then I noticed that the girl that was moving to this end seat, was wearing one of my dresses.

'That's my dress you're wearing,' I cried out.

'So what? You weren't here,' was the reply which got my rag and so I decked her, blotting my copy book. As she shook her head on the floor, I got my dress up over her body and heaved her up as I pulled it off of her.

'Nobody wears my clothes, ever,' I shouted at her and got some small satisfaction at seeing a trace of blood at her lip that she licked at as she looked up at me. There was fright in her eyes and I knew that they'd heard of Maureen and of how she finished up in hospital. The other girls had turned round to concentrate on the own reflections in the fly speckled mirror than look me in the eye at this sudden attack.

Sally had moved her make-up down to the third seat for me to have the second seat and I looked at the one that had taken my first seat and saw that she had a smug grin on her face.

'You can take that supercilious smile off your face,' I said to her, 'before I knock it off. Enjoy that seat while you can for you won't be in it much longer now that I'm back.' The grin disappeared and to give her credit, she kept her mouth shut and turned back to the mirror to continue to see to her make-up.

'Any chance of a drink, Sally? I've wound myself up too much,' I asked of her.

'Sure. Jean! Go and get a large gin and tonic for Jackie please,' she asked and the one that was second from the end got and went out and returned a couple of minutes later with a nice big glass full.

'Thank you Jean,' I said to the young thing that passed me the glass. Christ! I must be getting old when I'm thinking of these others as young things and I was only twenty years old myself. It seemed as though I'd been doing this for donkey's years and I stifled the thoughts of how I came to be where I was, though it was brought home to me a few days later - which we will come to in a moment.

Us six girls had to go out on stage and sing three songs each, with the girl nearest the door, the one that I'd clocked, starting the evening off. This gave me time to see that my face was as perfect as I could make it before I followed Sally's turn on the stage.

I got a lovely welcome from the regulars with shouts of, 'Nice to see you back, Jackie!' to which I shouted in return, that he saw my back more often than my front. It brought out a laugh with the others knowing that he fucked me quite often out in the cottages. 'We're rooting for you!' another cried out, to which I replied that he always had a root for all of the girls. That brought out more laughter. 'Give us your best!' one of the regulars shouted out, a cheer that only had one answer: 'That's for you to pay for out the back.' There was even more laughter after that, and then I went on and sang my three songs, finishing amidst tumultuous applause.

'Top that,' I said to the current queen bee as we passed on the stage and had the satisfaction that she didn't.

As we normally did when coming off stage, we circulated round the club to encourage the punters to buy us drinks at the exorbitant prices that were charged. As well as this, we were also selling ourselves and within a couple of minutes I was out in the cottages with one of them who almost slavered at the mouth when I said yes to his query. We didn't wear panties and the back of my dress was soon lifted as I bent over and had him push his throbbing cock up inside to fuck me. It cost him thirty quid to do that and I loved both the money and having a large prick again servicing me. I had another three fuck me before I had to return to the dressing room to check my make-up, having just earned in hours what I was paid for a whole week of singing.

After my next bout on the stage, I had two face fucks, having the man's cock in my mouth and taking his semen in and swallowing it and then telling him how lovely he tasted, though this service only cost them fifteen quid. The other two men I had fucked me nicely, thank you.

I kept getting told that it was nice for them to have me back singing again which bolstered my ego no end and I had another four men to round off the night, which was a financial success for me compared to giving it away for free in prison.

Such was the welcome I had been getting that night and for the rest of the week, our queen bee left and I was then back into the top seat and got top billing for the word went round that I was back and the place was full, as I was with cock every night both front and rear and loved every minute of it.

I had a shock during the next week, though, for I had a social worker call at the place I lived. I hadn't quite listened to what the judge had said when he'd sentenced me to three months inside, that I was to receive counselling because of my penchant for wearing female attire at all times whilst being of the male species.

I was shocked because if I'd known that she was coming I would have made myself up to the nines, but as it was, I wasn't in one of my best frocks nor was I wearing any make-up. For I would really have loved to have thrust myself into her face as to how good I did look when dressed to kill.

'Mr. Trent?' was the question asked in a rather doubtful tone by this woman at the door.

'Who's asking?' I countered.

'My name is Felicity Winters. I've been appointed by the court as your counsellor.'

'I beg your pardon?' I said, a little bewildered.

'It was mentioned at your trial that after serving your sentence, you are to spend at least six months with a counsellor and it has been given to me to see that this order of the court is obeyed. May I come in please?'

It was an automatic thing to open the door wider for her to enter as I tried to remember what it was the judge had said.

'The place is in a bit of a mess,' I apologized, 'I'm afraid I wasn't expecting any visitors.' I let her into my two roomed flat. It wasn't untidy but I could have at least plumped up the cushions on the settee and set aside the few magazines on the coffee table.

'Cozy,' said Miss Winters as she surveyed the sitting room, which was also my dining room. 'Do you live here alone?'

'Yes,' I snapped. 'Please sit down while I make myself a bit more presentable.' Not giving her time to reply, I left her and went into my bedroom. Bloody cheek, I said to myself as I quickly took off the frock I was wearing and put on a better and more suitable dress and sat down and put some make-up on. Looking at my reflection in the mirror, I smiled and said to myself, Now let's be the Christian and go out and face the lion. Now I felt girdled for battle. Well that's how it appeared to me, to be a battle of the sexes, though I was really more on her side than she knew.

'Coffee, tea or something else?' I asked of her when I returned to the sitting room, liking the expression on her face at me with my proper face on. 'I'm having a gin and tonic but the choice is yours,' I said sweetly and with a nice smile.

'Oh, er, coffee please,' she said.

'Ground, instant, espresso or cappuccino?' I asked, again with a sweet smile.

'Er, whatever's easiest,' she replied.

That would be instant, for I had neither the machine nor grinder for anything else, but, what the hell, she wouldn't know the difference anyway. One up to me, I chalked on my imaginary blackboard. I went and put the kettle on and while that was coming to the boil, poured myself a very large gin and splashed some tonic into the half full glass, letting her see just how much gin I poured into the glass. I nearly choked on it as it was that strong but kept the smile on my face.

'Now, what's this all about?' I asked and then jumped up before she could answer, exclaiming that the coffee was ready. I went and made it quite strong, only adding a little milk, and then brought it in on a tray with sugar as well as one spoon.

'Okay,' I said as I settled myself down with my drink while she sorted out the sugar with the spoon. 'Now why on earth should the judge think that I need counselling?' I knew the reason but I wanted to hear her version.

'Well Mr. Trent....' she began before I interrupted her.

'Jackie,' I said with my smile. 'I've always been called Jackie, ever since I was a little girl.'

'I beg your pardon, er, Jackie. Don't you mean a little boy?' she asked.

'Didn't I say that?' I asked in surprise.

'No. You said little girl.'

'Oh, maybe it's because I am a girl.'

'No you're not, Mr. Trent. You are a man!' she came back at me.

'How do you know that? Have you x-ray eyes and can see through my dress?'

'No, but you were sent to a men's prison,' she retorted.

'Yes, it was lovely to be surrounded by all those sex starved men. I had a ball.'

'But…but you were indicted as Mr. Jack Trent,' she stammered.

'I told them my name was Jackie Trent. I didn't, if you've read the court's transcript, admit to having the title of mister before my name,' I said, loving to see the consternation in her eyes.

'But in the prison…..' her voice trailed off.

'I had my back to them when I took of my dress and put on the male garments that were there for me to wear,' I said.

'But surely you were seen by a doctor before this?'

'No.'

'I don't understand that,' she said. 'You are a transvestite and no doubt a homosexual as well…..'

'Now that is slander, Miss Winters,' I said. 'Prove it!'

'You prove that you're a woman or a man first,' she countered.

'You show me yours and then I'll show you mine,' I said coyly but with a smile.

'This is getting us nowhere,' Miss Winters said. I got up from my seat and went over to where she was sitting on the settee and took hold of her hand and pushed it up to my crotch.

'Oh my God!' she exclaimed, her face going a bright red. 'You really are a man!' She snatched her hand back from mine as though she'd been burnt.

'Now that you've felt me, can I feel you to see if you really are a woman and not like me?' I asked, loving this little game.

'No you certainly can't!' she cried indignantly as she shrank back even further into the cushions of the settee.

'Ah well,' I sighed, 'you can't win them all. Is this what you came round for? To see if I am one or t'other?'

'Mr. Trent…..'she began before I interrupted her.

'You call me Mr. Trent once more and I will be showing you the door, via the toe of my right foot! The name is Jackie, haven't you understood this yet?' I thundered, almost spilling my drink in the process.

'I…I…I'm sorry, er, Jackie,' Miss Winters said, shrinking back on the settee again.

'Okay, apology accepted,' I said. 'Now please tell me the reason for this visit?'

'Well it's more to try and understand why, you who haven't been in any kind of trouble before, suddenly attack this woman in the pub?'

'Woman!' I snorted, rearing up again to make her cower back into her seat. 'That….that woman that you call her was Maureen Goodchild, a cross dresser like me! A man in drag, if you like. Though she's more of a tart and a slag to boot if you ask me. You're as bad as my solicitor, not getting your facts straight first. That "woman" was a man and didn't like me chatting up the man she wanted to have fuck her!'

You should have seen her face when I said this. Eyes wide and mouth open as her tiny mind took this information in. Whether it was by saying that Maureen was a man or saying the F word, I don't know. She looked as if she was lost for words.

'She fooled everybody like I fooled you into believing what you could see in front of you. I didn't know it was her tom that I was chatting up and when she hit me and tore my dress, well, that was it. Two bitches in heat fighting over a bone. The bone that he had between his legs that we both wanted to be fucked with. That was the reason for the fight. The fact that I hit the copper was because as I said at my trial, I didn't know it was one who grabbed my arm which was technically an assault for he hadn't made it known who he was behind as he grabbed me.'

'What about you kicking the other policeman, er, between the legs?' Miss Winters asked.

'That was pure frustration at being held as I was from behind and that that bitch Maureen was being treated as the victim when it was her that had attacked me first. I was only defending myself.'

'Like smashing a glass into her face?'

'All's fair in love and war,' I said. 'If you've ever been in a pub punch up before, you do your damnedest to put the other down first or you'll finish up having the shit kicked out of you. Survival is the name of the game out in this world, believe me.'

'But to smash a glass into her face,' she said, her eyes still wide.

'Oh for Christ's sake! Come out of your cocoon and see the real world that we live in. It's dog eat dog where I come from. None of you fucking do-gooders are ever going to change that!'

'Okay M...er, Jackie. I'm getting a better picture now that you've er, explained some of what actually happened. Which is the main reason that I am here.' She seemed to be getting her confidence back. 'Why, why did you appear in court dressed as a woman when you are a man? Why do you now wear a dress, even in your home?' she came out all in one breath, probably fearing I would interrupt her.

'Why, why, why?' I cried, getting up and storming across the room to get a fresh drink. 'Everybody has the same question on their lips, why. Why am I always being asked this imponderable question? Why this? Why that? The answer is that I don't fucking know!' I slammed myself back down into my chair and took a big swig from my glass.

'I've only asked so that I can try to understand you,' she said.

'Are you a trick cyclist?' I said, though it wasn't really a question.

'I've heard that expression used before, yes, I'm a psychiatrist.'

'I bloody well thought so,' I snorted into my glass but also was pleased to note that she had only taken a sip of her coffee and it would by now be cold. Chalk up another one for me, though I was now beginning to wonder how many points she was going to score off me.

'Look Jackie,' she said, coming forward to the edge of her seat, showing some spunk at last. 'I've not come here to either condemn or condone what you do, all I want to do is understand the why.'

'There it is again! Why? Why do you want, as you say, "to understand" me? To help me see the error of my ways? Surely that's the job of the Salvation Army?'

'Jackie, listen! Listen and hear what I've got to say instead of going off in these tirades. Just listen and help me to understand as to the way you feel and the reason behind your compulsive desire to keep dressing as a woman when you are, biologically a man.'

'Biologically? You've hit the nail on the head. What is biology but a knowledge of the composition of living creatures? But it never has and never will be able to completely understand the correlation between the brain and the heart. When man is able to do that, then maybe we'll all know the answers to what actually lies in the human psyche. It will then be able to tell me that though I've been given male genitalia why, that bloody word again, why I feel and act like a woman! So what do you propose?' I asked.

'I'd like to spend some time with you to just talk, well, for you to do the talking and for me to listen,' she said.

'I don't have a proper couch here,' I said.

'Don't be facetious, Jackie,' she admonished me. 'I'm only trying to learn of, of your er, sexual tendencies to try and help those people who are not as sure of their er, proclivities in the same direction. It would look good in my report if you agree to talk to me about this.'

'That sounds like a rather subtle threat of blackmail, Miss Winters,' I said.

'Well I can assure you that wasn't in my mind Jackie,' she said a little too haughtily to be believed.

'Okay,' I finally said after a few minutes' thought, 'but though this might be the place, it's not the time for I still have to work to pay the rent and eat,' I said sweetly. 'Also, if in agreeing to talk to you here, I will only do so as one woman to another. Do you understand that?'

'Perfectly, and I can then pass it on to my superior afterwards.'

'In that case then the answer is no. For either this is conducted as in a doctor's surgery or in a lawyer's office where what we speak about is treated in confidence, I will not say a word.'

'Okay, okay. I can assure you, Jackie, that whatever you say to me will be in complete confidence.'

'You'll be taking notes though,' I said.

'Yes but they will be locked away, I assure you.'

'If I ever find that you've lied to me, I'll sue you to your back teeth.'

With that, it was agreed that I would talk to her in my home at my time of choosing before she left and gave me time to have something to eat before going off to work.

I was back in my element as top of the bill and I sang my heart out and accepted the applause as well as the many invitations to visit the cottages for the purpose of being fucked. This is what it was all about for me, to have an erect male organ shoved up my back passage and revel in the power that was being used to not only give me pleasure but also to the punter who was paying for the privilege of fucking me. I would quite often come myself as I felt the other man's sperm hit my insides to coat it and make it easier for the next man to slide his cock up inside me. I could orgasm myself at least three times during one night of being fucked by so many hot throbbing cocks.

It was a few days after our first encounter that she called back at the flat for our first session of talking. She refused my offer of coffee which made me smile as I mixed myself a large gin and tonic and went and sat down on the settee for her to take the chair near me. I had dressed carefully and made sure that my make-up was perfect and I knew that if a man had walked into the room and saw us there, he would have been drawn to me first.

'Okay, I'm ready,' I said as I settled myself down comfortably on the settee.

'Alright, Jackie, but I must ask you to be truthful and not give me lies or any guff or it will be a complete waste of both our time and effort.'

'As long as you don't interrupt or be shocked at what you might hear,' I said.

'I promise,' she said as she sat there ready with her notebook. I took a big sip of my drink and lay back to answer her questions. At least she didn't start off with the word "Why."

She asked many questions, all of which I answered. The main thing being that I never really got on with my parents and would spend my summer holidays at my Aunt's house. She appeared to be somewhat of an invalid and was constantly looked after by her husband and I was left to myself. It was being alone that I began to experimenting on how I would look wearing female clothes in the gazebo in the garden.

They had a big standing mirror there, where I would put on the female things that I collected over time until I had what I wanted. I got such a thrill from donning these female items that I began to spend most of my time in there. I stopped having haircuts and let my hair grow long and in the end, on looking at myself in the mirror, I knew that if anyone could have seen me then, they wouldn't be able to say that I wasn't a girl.

That was it for the first session and as promised, Miss Winters returned the following week for us to carry on. I knew that she was not married for she wasn't wearing a wedding ring.

'So the question is do you want to continue in this, shall I say, the whys and wherefores of me wanting to stay always dressed as a woman?'

'I think I've bitten off more than I can chew, but yes, by all means, let us continue,' she replied.

'Are you a virgin?' I asked.

'What? My being a virgin or not has nothing to do with what we are discussing,' she said, a little red in the face.

'Oh yes it does,' I countered, leaning forward. 'I'm a virgin when it comes to whether or not I've had sex with a woman, but not one in the case of knowing a man. The reason for my asking is because if you are a virgin then you'll have no concept of what I'm talking about when I say that having a man's prick up inside you, feeling it throb and pulsate, knowing that he is going to spill his seed and in your case, get you pregnant if you're not on the pill, whereas in my case, it's a biological impossibility. If you've not had the experience of having a man fuck you, then you are wasting the time of both of us. Now, I'll ask you again: are you a virgin?'

'No,' she said in a low voice, her face quite red as she looked down at her notebook.

'Have you ever had sex with another female?'

'I…er, no.'

'Do you have any sexual feelings at all at seeing me dressed as you are and yet knowing that it is a man beneath the outer covering?'

'I…er, we're not here for me to answer your questions but you to answer mine,' she blurted out, her face now a flaming red and I noticed that she had to cross her legs, a sure sign that she had some kind of stirring within her. I gave her a sweet smile.

'I had hoped that there might be, what with me being a virgin in this sense and that you could possibly turn me into a heterosexual and lead me out of my life of depravity as you see it.' I gave out a big sigh and watched as she crossed her legs again. 'For with you crossing and uncrossing your legs like that shows me that you are getting rather wet between your thighs. Body language tells me a lot as well as your facial features. You do blush a pretty colour.'

'Please, Jackie!' she cried out. 'We're not here to discuss me, but you.'

'I know, but this is the very first time that I've sat down with a woman that has attracted me and you didn't really answer my question.'

'What question was that?' she asked, all flustered now.

'Was there any sexual curiosity as to what is under this dress, knowing that it is a man?' I then stood up in front of her.

'I...no,' she stuttered.

'You're not telling the truth now Felicity,' I said as I pushed the straps from my shoulders and let the dress drop to the floor, revealing myself in my ladies underwear and sporting a nice healthy erection.

'Oh my God! No Jackie, no,' she said, her eyes fixed on my throbbing penis as it swayed from side to side as I moved over to the settee and sat down beside her. 'This is not professional,' she said, seeming to have difficulty in getting these words out.

I put my arm round her shoulders and with the other hand, turned her face towards mine and pulled it close so that I could kiss her. She tried to mumble something as our lips met and I felt her shudder and lose some of the stiffness that I felt at first in her body. Her hand moved down and grasped my cock and she held it tight as we kissed.

With our lips now glued to one another, I let my hand go down and cup her breast and gently knead it as her body began to tremble and I didn't get any resistance when I pushed my hand between the buttons of her blouse and down into her bra to feel the real thing that was covered.

'Jackie, no,' she said without conviction as we broke off our kiss for breath. She made a halfhearted attempt to pull my hand out from her blouse but gave up when I kissed her again and now that arm came up to hold me as we did so. Her nipple was roused and now as hard as a little nut under the palm of my hand and her hand on my cock began to move on its own as she slowly began to rub me.

I released her breast and began to fumble and get the buttons of her blouse undone and soon was pushing it back over her shoulders. There was no resistance to this and none when I pushed the bra up for both of her breasts to fall free for me to massage and gently squeeze.

As if in slow motion, we slowly rolled and fell to the floor where she was forced to let go of my cock but this free hand came up to hold my head as we carried on with the kiss. I got my free hand to wander up her thigh, up on the inside of her skirt, and my fingers moved the gusset of her panties to one side and found that she really was wet. I pushed two fingers inside her.

She gave a gurgle and a slight squirm but made no effort to stop my questing fingers as they began to play with her clit.

We were both panting heavily now and she broke away from the kiss to quickly use her hand to pull off her panties and hoist her skirt up as I rolled over on top of her. The wetness between her thighs was like a flight guide path for my throbbing cock to home into the waiting field for me to land.

I moved over her more and slid into my first ever woman.

I reveled in the warm wetness that surrounded my cock, finding it softer and exerting less pressure than when inside the backside of a man. Also there were many more muscles that came into play to ripple along the length of my erection as I slowly eased myself in and out of her as we fucked there on the carpet of my sitting room.

Her legs came up to my waist and over my hips as I moved ever deeper inside her. It must have looked incongruous at this female clad body on top of another woman as the arse moved back and forth in the fucking motion. My first time of being inside a woman was blissful for the pressure on my cock was less intense, but there nonetheless.

'Oh God! And this is your first time?' she gasped out as we moved together.

'Yes,' I replied, making almost the same kind of noise that she was in between our gasps for breath.

'So…ooooh, don't stop. There…oooh, keep going, I'm coming,' she cried, her voice getting higher and then she convulsed under me, bucking like crazy, making me bounce even harder inside her. 'Now!' she screamed and held me in a vice like grip between her thighs as she shuddered, her back arching well clear of the floor, triggering me to come at the same time.

Both of us humping each other as we moved on the carpet as we came to our climax, her screaming and me crying out until we came to a shuddering halt and her hands came up and held my head tight as she fiercely kissed me.

Still on top of her though supporting some of my weight on my elbows, I stayed inside her as she flexed her muscles around my cock while I could only make mine twitch but it was enough for both of us know that it was still there.

'For a first time Jackie, that was one hell of a fuck,' she said and I don't know why but her use of the word "fuck" was the first time I'd heard her say it, and it surprised me though she'd already heard me use it quite often.

'For which I thank you very much, you being the first woman I've ever had the pleasure of being service to.'

'You can service me any time if it would be as good as this first time,' she said, her eyes alight and really glowing with pleasure.

'Well let's see how we can prolong these interviews we're supposed to be having,' I said, giving a peck on the end of her nose.

'Now you're talking dirty by mentioning work,' she said as she wrinkled her nose. It made me laugh and so I slipped out of her body, she giving out a little cry of dismay not unlike the ones I've often made when the cock that had been hard and fast up inside my backside was pulled out. I knew just how bereft she felt. This was another little piece that she could add to her slowly growing manuscript on the love life of a transvestite.

I rolled off of her and we had parted with the squelching sound of two sweaty bodies parting, a sound once heard and experienced is never forgotten. Her skirt was bunched up at her waist and her bra up around her throat, her legs wide open, her sex clearly visible and she was looking the veritable picture of a woman who had just been well and truly fucked.

I got up off the floor and helped her up and led her through to the bedroom where at least, I had a bathroom that led off of it. She was undoing the clip of her skirt as she went and that fell to the floor as did her bra just before she disappeared from view, her bare backside looking very nice indeed. It made me wonder if I could ever get to put my prick up in between those cheeks and fuck her that way as I would another man.

While she showered for a few minutes, I took off my underwear and as she came out of the bathroom, gave my shrunken prick a stroke as I went in for my shower. I was only in there a few minutes and when I re-entered the bedroom, found her still naked but now lying out on my bed. The only items that were incongruous in this attitude of hers was the fact that she had her pad and pencil with her.

'I thought that we were going to take it easy over the real reason for you being here,' I said on seeing these items.

'Let's get the story of your life out of the way first,' she said with a lovely smile that was much better that the previous ones I'd seen. Oh shit, I said to myself, for I'd seen that look before. Not on a woman I must say, but even on a man I recognized it was one of love.

Why?!

Why did this have to happen? The very first woman I had sex with, giving me this loving look! I was a confirmed homosexual and only loved having a male penis, up, erect and rampant, throbbing and having the expectancy of having it shoved up my arse. Now having fucked this woman was I going to have her as a mill stone round my neck? She patted the bed beside her and I, all meek and mild, did as I was bid and got onto the bed and lay down beside her. I had wanted to put on my underwear but she had stopped me from putting on my armour as what it seemed to me and now I was there naked on the bed with her and I felt so vulnerable at being in that condition.

'Now where were we before we got distracted?' she asked.

'Whether you were a virgin or not,' I said with a smile.

'Well that's been answered,' she said as she pushed my hand away from trying to get in between her thighs. 'Later.'

'Let's say that you were thinking of having me indicted for murder for a start,' I replied, now moving my hand up to a breast.

'Right, let's go on from there,' she said, all business-like now though it seemed strange to be continuing this with her lying naked there next to me and when the inevitable happened, there was nothing I could do about it for in my reminiscing, thoughts and scenes came to my mind and it wasn't long before I had a throbbing erection lying up on my stomach. But before this happened, I took up the story at near enough where I'd left off earlier. I did renege a little on what I really didn't want to say.

'While I stayed at my uncle and aunt's house in the summer,' I divulged, 'I quite often went into the village to do the shopping and it was there that I met a young boy and we seemed to get on really well together. So much so, that one day he told me, in secret, that he sometimes wore one of his sisters' clothes. He too was into dressing up as a girl and so I told him that I did the same. Well not his sister's clothes but my own that I had hidden in the gazebo which I eventually got him to come and see me when I was dressed as a girl. I even let him wear them sometimes and he, in the following year, brought the clothes of his sister up to the gazebo where we would both dress up and parade ourselves in front of the mirror.

'It was just before I arrived at the house that my uncle died,' I went on, 'and so I was there for the funeral and it was just after this, I got this boy whose name I'm not going to divulge, to come up to the house and introduced him to my aunt saying that this was a boy who I'd made friends with and would like, with her permission, to have him stay over some nights and be a companion for me. My aunt, sweet thing that she was, thought it good that I had made a friend of one of the villagers and so let him sleep over at least once a week.

'After breakfast, we would go down to the summer house and both dress up as women and then play at being lesbians. I found out that he had a good singing voice and as a surprise to me, found that I had a good voice too. We then got a record player down into the summerhouse and would, dressed as women, sing duets together. I, by now, hated wearing the constrictive attire of men, i.e. trousers and ties, and much preferred the loose flowing garments of a female.

'To please my aunt, who was quite good at the ivory keys, we would be in our normal boy's attire and sing while she played and really encouraged us in our singing and even got round to teaching us how to breathe properly when doing so. She did more for me in this field than my own parents ever did. They never really had time for me in all aspects of my childhood. I was there and that was it and I think they were glad to get rid of me every summer. Even when I had my sixteenth birthday and left school, they had no objections to me going off to live at my aunt's house, her agreeing to me moving in there as I would then be somebody to talk to of an evening ever since her husband had died.

'I loved those next two years of being able to discard trousers and the like to wear flimsy costumes and act and be a female in all senses of the word. I was in my element which I have since carried on to this present day. It wasn't until just after my eighteenth birthday that my friend and I, him being the same age as me, that we, when dressed as females in the gazebo, began to have sex together whilst dressed as girls. The difference being that underneath our dresses, we had erections that we could then suck on between us kissing each other that eventually turned to us fucking each other while dressed as women.

'Sodomy,' I explained, 'is the word used and that is the name given to the act of a male fucking another person up the arse and the person being fucked and liking it be it another male or a boy is called a sodomite. The one who receives the male cock instead of giving it was called a cat-amite. These words only came about from the Bible, but people like us were there long before Christ and before women became prostitutes, for a male whore was more valued than a woman over a thousand years before Christ.

'A catamite was a very much favoured person in any court and none more so than in Egypt. They were held in high esteem by the people who were fucking them and they rose to quite some powerful positions in their time. It had been learned that animals only copulated for procreation whereas humans joined together for pleasure too. The difference being that by a man going and fucking a catamite, didn't finish up with any unwanted offspring and possible threats to his reign as head of whatever position he held at the time.'

'You might lie there and espouse this,' Felicity interjected, 'but what you are talking about and saying that you do, is still against the law.' I snorted at this.

'The law? This only came about in the last two hundred years where people like me were doing this thousands of years ago and will con-tinue to do so till the world ends. There are many people who are, what we call "closet queens," hiding their sexuality in the closet. It is rife and can-not be controlled by any laws. We are talking about human nature and as soon as anything is banned by law, the problem it has tried to quell expands and grows all out of proportion.'

'Be that as it may,' Felicity said, 'It's still against the law.'

'God help us if they ban this,' I said as I rolled over onto my side and let her feel my erection pressing up tight to her thigh and caressed her breast. Her nipple rose up instantly into that tight little bud.

'God forbid,' she said as she pulled me over on top of her, her legs opening for me to get in between. She was wet and waiting and I slid in easily and fucked her to the pleasure of both of us.

***

Though it had been nice having Felicity, she would never replace a tight arsehole and neither could she give me what I really wanted, a big cock up mine. That was to be found at the club and it was nice to be up on the small stage again, singing and knowing that many of the men out there in the dark wanted me. They would give me what I craved and even paid me for it.

Coming off the stage after my third song, I would be given a drink. The regulars knew that it was a large gin and tonic for me instead of the muck they served up under the name of champagne. My leg would be stroked and I knew that he wanted me and so the drink went down in one and I would lead him to the cottages. Not until we were inside would I hold out my hand for the money and depending at how much he gave me determined whether it was oral or anal. Some of the men were fastidious enough to want a condom and this I would produce and expertly roll it down the erection that had been pulled out of the trousers. They varied from thick to thin, long to short but most were of the average size of about six and half inches.

I would bend over the basin in there and feel the hem of my dress lifted up to my waist as a hand held it up on my hip as his other hand guided him to where he wanted to go. It was lovely to feel the head of the cock nuzzle my entrance and then have it pushed in, widen me to fit him as he would slide into me as his other hand now held my other hip. Then it was chocks away and I would be flying as the man behind me started to move and drive his cock in as far as he could as he fucked me. His thighs, covered by his trousers, would press to the cheeks of my arse on his forward ramming and sometimes nearly pull out in his motions. Not many men lasted more than a minute of moving his cock in and out of me till he gripped my hips tighter as he pulled me close to him and began to jerk out his sperm into the rubber or me. It was glorious and I could never get enough of this pleasure.

Very seldom were we alone out there for there was nearly always one or more of the other girls being serviced in this way or down on their knees giving their trick a blow job. How we finished half of our shows I don't know for we were nearly always half pissed by the time the finale came having had quite a few drinks tossed down our throats.

The week flew by and I soon had Felicity knocking at the door to my flat once again. She gave me a smile and a peck on the cheek as she entered and now being familiar with the place, went straight over to where the drinks were and poured us both out a drink.

'Shall we take these into the bedroom with us?' she asked and without waiting for an answer, went ahead of me. After taking a sip of her drink, she put the glass down on the bedside table.

'Get that dress off then,' she said as she slipped the straps off her shoulders and let hers fall to the floor. It was off quicker than mine and I saw that she was wearing just the same as me, a bra, suspender belt and stockings and no panties.

There were two differences between us as we faced each other, both quite beautiful to look at but she was able to fill her bra and be seen to do so which I couldn't and I had a straining erection jutting out from my thighs where her flat tummy ran straight down to her small bush without any protuberances.

'It's a lovely shape,' she said as her fingers ran down the top of my shaft and she went down onto her knees as her hand grasped the base of my cock and put her mouth over the head. The inside of her mouth was hot and her tongue flicked over and round the head as she gave me some sucks while working her hand up and down on me.

'Not too much,' I groaned, loving to see her brunette hair weave about as she bobbed up and down on me.

'No,' she said, letting go of me and standing up and moving back towards the bed. 'I want it to come inside me, but first, give me a lick and a suck.' She now laid back on the bed and opened her legs for me to see what she wanted me to attend to with my mouth and tongue.

Now I'd already had my cock stuck in there between those lips but never really looked at a real live one before. I'd seen pictures but not close up as I now was and I must say that it's not the best view in the world. There was nothing to really get hold of with either hand or mouth, not like a rampant cock that you could feel properly, and it was not something that you could use your teeth on. With a woman it was mostly the tongue to be used and to me, it'll never take the place of giving head to another man. I didn't stay down there long and I soon moved up and pushed myself into what I'd just been tickling and got more pleasure this way though I would still rather it had been a man. But a hole is a hole and a fuck is a fuck so I did the best I could with what I had.

It must have made a good picture viewed from the side to see two female clad people together, one on top of the other and it would have been hard to tell which was which as I was squashing her breasts with my chest. Though it was her that cried out in the throes of an orgasm while I just grunted away as I came inside her.

The difference was also apparent when I pulled out and moved back onto my heels, my wet cock still pulsating as it stuck out from my thighs. As exhausted as she looked, Felicity still turned round on the bed and took my cock into her mouth and sucked on me for several minutes as I stroked her hair not knowing that this was the last time I was going to see my psychiatrist. There was no hint of this as we got dressed again and she gave me a kiss before leaving.

But for some reason or another, it was the last time we had sex together though we did meet again later in the year. I didn't really miss having sex with her for I was getting banged regularly every night in the club and putting my money away for a rainy day. I didn't expect it to be a storm a week later.

It started with Bambi Bambridge, the first name being taken from the surname. He, she was only eighteen and was quite fussy about who she would let fuck her out in the cottages. Well there was one man who had wanted her and didn't like being rebuffed by her during her turn at circulating among the tables. I can't say that I noticed this during my forays out into the crowd for my usual fucking and it was after our nightly show was over that it happened.

Two of the girls, Sally being one of them, had a regular boyfriend that would wait for them to get their stage make-up off before leaving the club. I was just in front of these four as we left the club, Bambi had been a minute or two before me and as I stepped out into the street, I saw her fall to the ground after being hit by this man that had pestered her all night. He gave her a kick while she was on the ground and then dragged her half upright by her hair to hit her again when I shouted out and grabbed his arm. He let go of her and swung round without me knowing he had a knife in his hand. I got this sudden pain in the side of my neck that almost paralysed me with shock.

I couldn't scream out as he pushed me backwards to the ground as the other two men following behind me with their girls stopped him from going any further. This rest was related to me later by Sally who was first at my side as I lay on the road, choking and coughing up blood from my throat. She was screaming as she stuffed the hem of her dress to the wound at my neck that was pouring with blood. The attacking man managed to get free of the other two men and ran off with one chasing, but didn't catch up with him.

As the other man leaned over Bambi, Sally screamed out at him to get an ambulance, fast. She thought I was bleeding to death, thinking that by the amount of blood, the attacker may have caught the jugular vein.

With any luck, he hadn't, but there was still a lot of blood which she was trying to staunch.

I was out and unconscious during this and she sat there on the ground with me, holding her dress up to my neck, pressing as hard as she could. Her man had called for an ambulance from the club and also the police who arrived first, a good five minutes before the ambulance. They thought that three of us had been hurt at first because Sally was now all covered with blood and Bambi was still unconscious too. There was little they could do until the ambulance arrived and the paramedics took over. Sally came with the two of us in the ambulance while her man stayed behind to relate what happened to the police.

I was taken straight into emergency and within fifteen minutes was on an operating table where I lay for two hours while surgeons battled to save my life. I was on the critical list for two days and it was only my youth and resilience that kept me in the land of the living.

The knife I had been struck with had missed the jugular artery but had cut into my vocal cords and this is what kept me on the operating table so long as they tried their best to stitch these together. It was nearly two weeks before they told me that the operation wasn't a hundred percent successful and though I would eventually be able to speak, my singing career was over. I was lying there with tubes up both nostrils as well as one down my throat and heavily bandaged around my throat and couldn't help the tears that began to flow from eyes at this news. Sally, who'd spent as much time as she could with me, cried with me as she held my hand tight, telling me that being alive was the most important.

Which didn't help me for singing was my life! It meant that I couldn't sing in the club and have many men fuck me and if I couldn't sing there, how was I going to get my regular supply of hard cocks. This was the hardest thing to bear and I just couldn't stop crying and almost had a relapse because of it.

But they pulled me through this darkest period of my life to date and I vowed that somehow I was going to get myself back together to get out and find men. I could only write notes as I recovered and I asked Sally through this medium if they had found the man who had knifed me. No was the answer, which didn't surprise me, but his face was forever etched in my brain as he'd swung his arm up at me. I would get him one day even if I had to scour the whole country. Why oh why did this have to happen to me?

It was two weeks before the doctors let the police sit by my bedside to ask me questions. Sally was allowed to stay with me but mustn't interrupt as she'd already given her version of the attack and she would read out my answers. I think she enjoyed this.

Q. Why did this man attack you?
A. Because I got in the fucking way
Q. The way of what?
A. Him kicking and punching the shit out of Bambi.
Q. By Bambi, do you mean Mr. Bambridge?
A. If that is Bambi's surname, yes.
Q. Do you know the name of this man that attacked you?
A. No.
Q. Why was he attacking Mr. Bambridge?
A. Because Bambi wouldn't let him fuck him.
Q. By that, do you mean he wanted to have anal sex with Mr. Bambridge?
A. What fucking planet do you live on? Where the fuck do you think the prick wanted to stick his prick? In her ear? Maybe that's what you need to get some sense into you instead of asking these stupid fucking questions.

***

'**Now, there's no** need to come out with words like that, Mr. Trent,' the copper said.

'Then fuck off, I'm tired,' I wrote and Sally spoke for me as I lay back on the pillows and closed my eyes.

'Okay, Mr. Trent. If you think of anything that may help us, send us word,' he said. I mouthed the words for him to fuck off and I heard the scraping of chairs as they got up and left my room.

'They've gone,' Sally said and I opened my eyes and smiled at her. 'That was great, telling them to fuck off.' Her eyes were smiling as she said this but I could also see that there was tiredness in them and wrote on the pad that she shouldn't come every day for she needed rest too. She objected but her heart wasn't in it for she knew that I'd written the truth.

I had one other special visitor and that was Bambi. She called me a silly bitch for getting involved but thanked me in the same breath for my intervention. It was nice to see the odd girl from the club drop in but they soon tired me out and I wrote out my thanks but asked them to let me rest and get better.

Three weeks later I had a second operation now that I was over the first one. This was to make more repairs to my larynx. It was another two months before I came off the intravenous feed and was given my first solid food since entering the hospital, though solid is not the right word for thin soup. I was also encouraged to try and speak and the first effort hurt my throat and all that came out was a croak that made me cry, but I persevered and found that I could actually make noises that were real words.

My voice was lower and more husky, much like Joan Greenwood and Fenella Fielding, two actresses that I admired for their sexy tones. It would take a little getting used to but the main thing was that I could now speak and be understood instead of having to write out all that I wanted to say.

I did have one other visitor in the hospital and it was Miss Winters, who told me that she would be my social worker again until I was fit enough to face the world once more. She arranged for me to be visited by a therapist and having visions of what she and I had once done together, I said yes. I didn't know she was taking about a speech therapist who, after speaking to me and treating me as though I were a child, I soon sent packing.

Sally was with me when the time came for me to leave the hospital after spending nearly four months there. I thanked the doctors and nurses for their care and attention and had to suffer to be taken home in a wheelchair, still wearing the hateful gown that had no back to it. But that was hospital practice and as soon as we entered my flat I got out of the wheelchair and took off the robe and gown and threw them onto the seat.

Oblivious of the two ambulance men still there, I strode naked over to my drinks cabinet and poured myself out a large gin and tonic and nearly choked on this first decent drink for nearly four months. By Christ did it burn my throat but it really warmed my stomach and turning round, offered the two men a drink which they politely refused.

They left after I thanked them and offered Sally a drink which she accepted and we clinked our glasses together.

'Thank you Sally for all the time you've spent with me at the hospital and there is only one thing left for me to ask of you,' I said as we drank.

'What's that?' she asked.

'Take me to bed and fuck me for I've been dying to have a cock for God knows how long.' I said it with a smile and she readily agreed and so to bed we went. I was already naked and got onto the bed and watched her take her clothes off and saw that she was up and ready and I said to forget the condom as I wanted to feel all of her as she was inside and of her coming too.

It was lovely to have a cock plough my furrow again and I drooled at the pleasure almost forgotten and urged her to fuck me harder. This Sally did until she strained and began to jerk as she came inside me. She staggered off to the bathroom to wash as I relived and savoured that warm glow in my stomach at having been fucked again. I would have liked going down on her and sucking her cock but I would have to leave the pleasure of oral sex for a while until my throat had really healed properly, so I fucked her instead.

Sally left soon after for she had to go to work at the club, leaving me alone in the silence of my room, missing the bustle of nurses. I cried that night in bed. No job because I couldn't sing which meant no men to fuck me and pay for my rent and food and the money I had saved for a rainy day wouldn't last forever. I was really miserable and rather short tempered when I got my visit from Miss Winters. She misunderstood my mood thinking it was because of my loss of singing ability and my job, not of the men that I craved to have behind me or in my mouth.

My second week in my flat became a living hell for I couldn't stand the inane programmes being put out on the television and I couldn't concentrate on reading books and magazines. So I would spend a lot of that time just walking about the streets to tire myself out so that I could sleep at night.

I had been out walking and began to feel hungry and so I went back to the flat and got a shock when I opened the door and went through into the sitting room. For sitting there was none other than Eddie Forbes, with a big smile on his face.

'Surprise!' he said.

'It sure is. Why are you here? You've still got eight more years to serve,' I said. He got up and put his hands on my shoulders and half turned me to look at the scar at the side of my throat.

'I'll tell you later. How are you feeling? I read about what happened to you and I just had to come and see if you are alright.' The question was asked sincerely for I could see it quite plain on his face.

'You've broken out of prison! You didn't just break out to come and see me?' I asked incredulously.

'No,' he said with a laugh. 'The opportunity arose for a break out and so I took it. To come and see you was a combination of three things.'

'Sex, sex and sex again, is what springs to mind,' I said with a laugh.

'Well, that was one of the three,' he laughed. 'Another was to see if you were alright and if there was anything I could do and the other, well, I need a place to lie low for a little while until I can get out of the country.'

'Well to the second question the answer is I'm fine. Though I can't sing anymore, I'm still alive. As to the other two questions, the answer is yes. You can stay here as long as you like for it's been a long time since I've had a man such as you. You don't get what you can give me from the National Health Service.' He laughed and I broke free from his hands and went and poured out some drinks for us, him preferring whisky.

We'd only sat down with our drinks when there came a knocking at the front door. Both of us were startled at this and then I remembered that it was the day for Miss Winters to call.

'Oh Christ! It's my social worker. Quick! Into the bedroom and don't make a sound,' I said to him and made sure he took his glass with him before he closed the door for me to then go and let Miss Winter in.

She refused my offer of a drink seeing that I'd already started but accepted a cup of coffee. We spoke for several minutes, me bringing up the subject on collecting unemployment benefit, asking that the six-week period be waived as I was in hospital at the time and unable to sign on. This she said she would see to and that we should meet at what used to be called, the Labour Exchange to sort out getting me some form of monies. We were talking of this when there came another knock at the door and excusing myself, went and opened the door to find two plain clothes police officers. They asked if they could step inside and so I let them in.

I introduced them to Miss Winters who told them who and what she did and why she was there and then asked why were they here?

'A felon escaped from Wandsworth Prison in the early hours of the morning, one Eddie Forbes. He's on the run and we are checking out the likely places he might seek sanctuary.'

'So why pick on me?' I asked.

'We were given to understand that you were his woman whilst you were in there, Mr. Trent,' one of them said, laying heavy emphasis on my name and title considering I was dressed as a woman in my own flat.

'Just because he fucked me a couple of times while I was there isn't a very good reason why he should come here,' I said quite haughtily. 'If, as you are alluding, I was one of his known associates, this would be one of the places to avoid for that very reason. He'd be bloody stupid to come here and I can assure you he isn't stupid by any means. Miss Winters, does this mean that because I once went to prison I'm going to be subjected to this for the rest of my life?'

'I should hope not,' she said and then went on for several minutes berating the two men on how it was more of a misunderstanding that I had finished up in prison and that she had no doubt as to my integrity as an honest citizen who has since been the victim of a crime of more violence and that they, the police, have yet to apprehend the man who had inflicted such damage on myself. She was bloody good and when she'd finished with them, I invited them to check out the flat which they declined to do and soon left, though telling me it was my duty to inform them if he tried to make any contact with me.

'I'll be as diligent as you,' I assured them as I showed them out. 'Can you believe the bloody cheek of them?' I exclaimed to her when I returned to the sitting room. 'I clobber a copper by mistake and get thrown inside and when I'm nearly killed, they do nothing and expect me to harbour an escaped prisoner? Well I would if it came to that, but as I said, this would be one of the last places he would come to.' I went and refilled my glass and sat down again.

'Did I understand the man right when he said that you had been this man's woman inside, that you had sex with him?' she asked, her eyes not exactly wide, but enough for me to know that she wanted a little bit of gossip.

'Yes,' I confessed. 'He used to fuck me.'

'Why?'

'It was for my own protection. Those others inside would very soon have known who and what I was and rather than be gang raped by ten or more inmates as and when they pleased, it was better to offer myself to just one man and therefore be protected from the depredations of the others. Do you understand the logic of this? If you don't, then I suggest you spend a little more time in finding out exactly what goes on in the prisons, and that also includes the female ones too, for they can be real bitches too.'

'Well you've certainly given me a lot to think about, Jackie. Now it's about time I was going. Now don't forget to let them know if this man tries to contact you.'

'If he calls upon me from now, I most certainly will,' I assured her. The fact that he already had meant that I was not telling any lies at that very moment as I showed her out and thankfully shut the door. I went to my bedroom to be engulfed in Eddie's arms and kissed.

'You were wonderful,' he said between kisses. 'I heard every word and nearly shit bricks when you invited them to look around.'

'I knew what I was doing,' I said. 'They'd already been put down and weren't going to have it done again especially without a search warrant.'

'How can I thank you?' he asked to which I think you know the answer.

'Put me on the bed and fuck me,' I said which he promptly did and it was like welcoming home an old friend to have his cock slide up inside me and blow my brains out with his coming, making me come at the same time without using my hands.

It was nice to lie in his arms again after being sexually satisfied with knowing the added benefit that I would be able to sleep in the same bed with him that coming night unlike while being in prison. There, I had to be in my own cell with Bert, but tonight, he would be all mine to have and to hold and have his strong arms round me as I slept.

I had enough food in the flat for a couple of days at least and over our evening meal he, well not exactly, told me of his escape. He wouldn't go into specific details for he said the less I knew the better, besides, he might need to use the same means again, he said with a smile. But his main concern was if he could continue to stay in my flat until he had the means to leave the country. Though the rider was if I would be his go between to set all this in motion? Of course I said yes, though the longer I could keep him in the flat, the more sex I would get was the main thought that ran through my mind.

It was nice to go back to bed and see his naked body which I hadn't seen whilst in prison and that he was extremely fit and he looked more powerful when he was naked with a steaming erection that I knew was for me alone and how I really longed to go down onto my knees and take him into my mouth. But as I was going to get it anyway, I had to content myself with just kissing and licking the head of his cock before putting a condom on and getting onto the bed and feel his hands once again on my hips. Then came the pleasure of feeling him push the head of his cock up to my arsehole and slip inside and have the rest of his shaft fill me and have him pulsate there before reaming my canal. I was back in heaven for I knew that he was mine, albeit for a short time, and I intended to make the most of the time he would be living with me.

To keep his strength up, read that as his cock, he needed to be well fed and this needed money, which he gave me the means to get as I passed on messages at the same time. Now I didn't know his associates in the part of the world that they lived though it was within one mile of the club for I'd had no reason to do so in the past. But I soon became aware of this underground means of living and operating outside of the law. Bert Wilson, my old cell mate had been released while I was in hospital and I was to use him to make contact with Eddie's men.

The pub was in Whitechapel which I'm not going to name for obvious reasons, where I would pick up Bert who would then introduce me to others who would help both me and Eddie. I couldn't have had any better therapy to get me out of my doldrums than acting as this liaison between Eddie and his cohorts.

I took to wandering around the Whitechapel area, stopping in different pubs in case I was being followed until I met up with Bert. From him I got a kiss on the lips when we did finally meet, which looked natural in spite of the age difference because I went out as I usually did, dressed as the woman I always believed I was.

'You're a sight for sore eyes,' Bert said as he gave me a hug. 'After reading about what happened to you in the newspaper we get, I prayed for you, I really did.'

'Thank you, Bert. When did you get out?'

'Two months ago and right glad to, I can tell you, for it wasn't the same after you left. I got a right turd shoved in with me. Nowhere as clean and honest as you.'

'Thank you Bert,' I said as I gave him a kiss on the cheek and accepted the offer of a drink.

'Have you heard the latest?' he gushed as soon as we had sat down.

'About Eddie Forbes, yes, I have,' I replied with a smile knowing that I was going to drop a bombshell on him. 'That's why I've come looking for you.'

'For me? Why?' That everlasting question.

'To see if you could help him,' I said simply.

'Help? Of course I would. It was because you was my cell mate that he looked after me after you was released. Though he couldn't do much about the shit that was put in with me but he made sure that he toed the line with me. I just hope that he stays free and gives them all a lot of bother of finding him.'

'That he'll do all right for they won't find him,' I said quite assuredly.

'How can you be so sure, Jackie?'

'Because I know where he is and am now asking you to help me get him out of the country,' I said.

'Well bugger me!' he breathed.

'That's my line,' I said dryly. 'Now he came to me to ask you to become a go-between with his old mates and pass on messages and the like but pass them through me. Do you think you can do that? I don't know them and it would look suspicious if I start ferreting around.'

'Of course I will,' he said, his eyes alight. 'What does he want?'

'The first thing is to let them know that he's in a safe hiding place. The second is for some cash and thirdly, a false passport. Now he trusts me and I've vouched for you and he wants you to be very careful and only speak to one of his cronies so that if anything goes wrong, he'll know who to go looking for if it does. Make this quite clear at the outset or we'll both end up back in there and I can't guarantee that we'll be put back in the same cell together.'

'Don't worry on that score Jackie, but, you know, I missed you when you left. Then to hear of your trouble and I wished that I could have been out there to help you. If there's anything that I can do, in, er, well, er, you might, er…..'

'Say no more, Bert,' I said with a smile. 'Come out back with me.'

I stood up and had him follow me out into the passage where the toilets were. 'We'd better use the ladies,' I said as I pushed open the door and went in with him behind me. Well that's where he wanted to be and I wanted him there too. Not having seen any women in the pub, we knew we wouldn't be disturbed and I lifted up the hem of my dress and bent over by the sink and he quickly pulled himself out of his trousers and I had the pleasure of once more having Bert's thick, though slightly shorter prick shoved up my arse to give me a good fucking. He enjoyed having me as much as I enjoyed letting him and feeling his seed spurt out into me as he came quite prolifically.

'Oh God I missed this with you, Jackie,' he said, pumping away as he came, thighs tight up to my backside as he jerked in his outpouring.

'I missed having you too, Bert,' I gasped as I came all over the inside of my dress at the same time. I gave a little cry as he pulled out, leaving a vacuum in my backside and knew that as soon as I let air get back inside it would want to come back out in the form of a fart. That eventually happened but it wasn't loud enough to be noticed as he washed his cock at the basin and dried it on paper towels before putting it away.

We then agreed to meet again in two days' time for him to tell me how he got on with Eddie's pals. I went back home quite happy at having had a fuck and that it was Bert and that he had agreed to help in Eddie's escape to freedom.

Of course Eddie wanted to know all that I'd done, which wasn't much really and told him that I'd made contact with Bert, omitting that I'd let him fuck me and so I got Eddie to do the same and so I was a really happy bunny as I made dinner that night. For there was more to come in both senses of the word and I got my fair share of Eddie's when he fucked me again that night in bed.

I think I fretted more than he did during the following day, hoping that Bert had made contact but not do too much in aiding Eddie's escape from the country for I liked having him in my bed. I got carried away as I lay there, kissing, licking and gently nibbling on his erection, so much so that I took him into my mouth to suck and tease him and couldn't help myself but carry on until he came with a surge for me to take it in and eventually swallow it and finding that I could still at least manage to do this without harming my throat.

I had tried to do some singing but found that it was nigh on impossible and it really hurt my larynx in the trying. So I was pleased that this was something that I still could do, something that gave me the same pleasure as having one stuffed up my backside.

I met with Bert the next day and he passed to me one hundred pounds for Eddie's immediate expenses.

'These are not forged notes, are they?' I asked of him.

'No. I can assure you they are genuine. They came from the last bank they robbed.' I couldn't help but laugh at this as I put it away. 'I had a job convincing them that it was for Eddie. The man I talked to wanted to know who I was in contact with but I wouldn't tell.'

'Who was this man?' I asked.

'Him at the bar, Daniel Tanner.'

'Oh for Christ's sake Bert!' I hissed at him. 'He's followed you and saw you give the money to me so now he knows!'

'Oh. Sorry, Jackie. I didn't think,' he said in a crestfallen voice.

'Never mind Bert, it's done so I'll have to think for a minute,' I said as I ran a few things through my mind and decided to take the bull by the horns. 'Bert. Ask this Mr. Tanner to join us and bring over some fresh drinks, please. Though wait a moment. Don't mention my name whatever you do.'

'Okay Ja…. er, Miss,' he smiled at me as he got up. I watched him order the drinks and talk to the man, indicating me and when he was served, came over with the drinks and the man in tow.

'This is the young lady who wishes to speak to you,' he said to Tanner as they both sat down and I was passed my drink.

'So you know where Eddie is hiding out, Miss……?'

'I do, Mr. Tanner and I'm not about to divulge that information to a stranger,' I replied.

'I'm not a stranger to Eddie. We're almost like brothers,' he said.

'Well that I will find out in a couple of days' time when I next see Eddie.'

'A couple of days?'

'He moves around and only contacts me when he wants to,' I replied with a smile. 'Now what about his passport?'

'It will be sorted out if I know that you're acting for him,' he said.

'Do you trust Bert?'

'Yes.'

'So does Eddie, and you've trusted Bert enough to give him a hundred pounds and he trusts me to hand it over,' I said.

'What visas does he want in the passport?'

'I don't know. He'll probably tell me when I pass this on. You don't trust me, do you? I can see it in your eyes.'

'No I don't,' he said truthfully. 'When you see Eddie, ask him what is his married sister's middle name. If you give me the right answer next time we meet, I'll then trust you.' he said as he finished off his beer and got up and left the table.

'Distrusting bastard,' I said in a low voice to Bert.

'He's being as careful as you are. It was me that fucked this one up,' he said mournfully. 'Just take care that there isn't another one outside who might try to follow you,' he advised. I told him I would as I finished my drink and promised to look in again in a few days' time and I left the pub.

After taking two taxis and two buses and getting myself lost in Selfridges, I finally made my way home ninety-nine percent sure that I wasn't followed on the last stretch.

'Here's ninety pounds,' I said to Eddie after getting a welcome home kiss, something I could get used to. 'I spent ten quid just to make sure that I wasn't followed by one Daniel Tanner.'

'You met Dan?'

'Yes, and I only got the money because he trusts Bert, but I don't think he trusted me. He asked me to ask you what is your married sister's middle name.' He burst out laughing.

'You're right. He doesn't trust you. He knows that I've got one sister and she's not married and her middle name is Mildred. You can also tell him that I know that his mother never married his father,' to which he went off on another laughing bout. 'That'll show him that you are for real for it's something that he's kept hidden for years. Now what else was said?'

'What visas do you want in the passport?'

'Hmmm. Now why does he want to know that?' he mused which told me that he didn't really trust this Tanner that much either, but I kept my mouth shut. 'Tell him no visas but just make sure that it has a few European entry and exit stamps in it. Also I will want twenty grand and a driving license in the same name as what's in the passport.'

'Are you sure he'll come up with all this?' I asked, my hand straying down to stroke his crotch.

'If he doesn't, he'll miss out on a hundred grand for only I know where the money's buried from the last job,' he said with a cackle and I felt his body start to respond to my hand movements.

'So if he fucks you about, he's fucked but in a different fashion as how I would like to be fucked with what I can feel?'

'That's about the size of it,' he said laughing at his pun as he pulled his erection out of his trousers for me to go down on him. Being face fucked is another way that I like being seen to and enjoyed the power I had to make the man come and fill me with his sperm to taste, savour and swallow and then slyly kiss him with a trace of his own coming still on my lips.

The week passed too quickly for me and I had the usual visit from Miss Winters who asked how I was coping and I told her just fine now I was getting some unemployment benefit and would give myself another few weeks before starting to look for another job. Yes, my throat was feeling much better and it didn't hurt as much now for my speaking though still regretted that I could no longer sing. There was no mention of the police by her as Eddie stayed in the bedroom during her visit which lasted for an hour before she left.

The next day I went and found Daniel Tanner with Bert and I rounded on Tanner.

'So much for Eddie's sister being married when she isn't, and her middle name is Mildred. So do you trust me now?'

'Yes, but you still haven't told me your name and Bert won't tell me.'

'As Eddie trusts me I suppose you will too after I tell what else Eddie told me to say to you.' I leaned in right close so that I could whisper in his ear. 'That you are also a bastard.' I leaned back with a smile on my face at the look of shock on his.

'Don't ever repeat that,' he said with a grim look on his face now.

'So don't you ever let slip my name either then. It's Jackie. Jackie Trent.' A puzzled look came over his face.

'I've seen that name somewhere, but just can't recall it at this minute.' I pulled down the edge of the collar of the blouse I was wearing and let him see the scar which was still quite a vivid red. 'Oh yes,' he breathed out. 'The girl who was stabbed outside that transvestite club.' Then he looked at me again with a hint of surprise in his eyes. 'You're a transvestite?' I nodded, him not having twigged that I wasn't a female after two visits.

'Well, well, well. Eddie's fucking a queer!' I upped and slapped him hard round the face which was a shock both to him and Bert for me to do that.

'Don't ever call me that,' I snarled at him, 'or I'll do the same to you that I'm going to do to the cunt that knifed me when I find him.' I think he was too shocked at me slapping him for him to really know what to do or say next.

'Sorry, Jackie. Can you describe the man who did this to you?' he asked for want of anything else to say for it would have looked bad for him to slap a female in this pub. This I could do in detail and he looked pensive when I'd finished.

'Three, maybe four men could fit that description. I'll check them out for you. Now, what about Eddie's passport?' I told him about no visas but a couple of European stamps inside and the money. 'Okay. I'll have the passport by next week, the money will take about two weeks to get together.'

This would have to do and I passed this on to Eddie and I met them both the following week and was given the passport which I put into my bag and then was surprised when he brought out onto the table a digital camera and clicked through pictures of six men.

'Any of these?' he asked. 'They all fit your description.'

'Yes. The fourth one. That was the man that knifed me,' I said.

'What do you want us to do with him?' So I told him and he said he would arrange it for the next week.

I urged Eddie to be brutal in his fucking of me that night for I wanted to try and wash away the pain and agony I had gone through because of that man and couldn't wait till the following week. We met up in the pub and he told me that they had the man in a small lock up garage for me and he had admitted that it had been him that attacked both Bambi and myself. He also passed across to me a bag that contained the money for Eddie before we left the pub and I was driven to where they had got the man that had knifed me.

I was led in by Daniel and there were two others of his gang if they could be called that and the man I wanted most was there too. He'd been stripped naked and was tied in an almost crucified fashion to some sturdy racking and I could see that he'd been beaten and tortured. His chest and nipples had cigarette burns and his stomach was showing signs of bruising.

'Did he have his knife with him?' I asked, and it was given to me and I found that the edge was sharpened like a razor. 'So he admitted that it was him though I know just by looking at his face that it was.'

'Yes,' said Daniel. 'He admitted it, finally.' The man had been gagged so he wouldn't be able to scream at what I was going to do to him for my blood was now boiling up at just seeing that face again and his eyes were wide open in fear at seeing me there before him with his own knife.

'Okay,' I smiled thinly at the man. 'Leave us alone so there are no witnesses to what I'm going to do to him.'

'Right, Jackie. We'll clean up the mess afterwards,' Daniel said as he ushered the other two men out and left me alone with the man who'd ruined my life by stabbing me in the throat. The man was trembling as he looked at me, especially when I lifted up his knife for him to see the light flash off the blade.

'I'm not a sadistic person. Though I would just love to cut you up into little pieces, I'll be quick. But you will suffer as I did.'

I then reached out my hand and took hold of the head of his penis and pulled it out straight. 'You wanted to fuck Bambi with this and because she wouldn't let you, you stabbed me. Well you're never going to be able to fuck anyone from now on,' I said as I brought the knife down close to his stomach and sliced right through his prick and quickly stepped back with it in my hand as blood began to spurt out from where his cock had been attached to his body. I heard him scream through his gag as his body writhed against the ropes that held him up and his head then slumped forward as he passed out.

I was surprised at how easy the sharp blade of the knife had sliced through the flesh and muscle of his penis and I now stuck the tip of the blade through it and walked away from his tied up body and stuck the knife with his prick into the wooden door as I went out.

'He's all yours now,' I said to Daniel who was waiting outside with the others. 'I'm afraid there's a bit of a mess in there. I'm going home now,' and I left them to sort him out.

Eddie was pleased to see me and the money and gave me big kisses but sensed that something was wrong and so I told him that I might have just killed a man and told him what I had done. I cried now for myself at how vicious I had been and wondered if it had been worth it.

I had killed him for it was in the newspapers two days later that a naked body had been fished out of the Thames. The dead man had been tortured before being mutilated, it didn't say exactly how, and his body thrown into the water and it had been found that he'd died from the loss of blood and not by drowning. His name hadn't been mentioned and I wondered if the police would ever find the link between us. Daniel and his men had obviously known they couldn't just take him to a hospital with his dick missing and so had dumped him into the river.

But I still cried and Eddie consoled me by making love to me in our fashion and saw to me twice within an hour finding some superhuman strength to do this in so short a space of time. He also fucked me twice that night in bed as he told me that he would be leaving in the morning and thanked me for sheltering him and that sometime in the future, I would receive a postcard to let me know where he was and that I was to destroy it straight away.

We woke up early the next morning and I had him fuck me one last time and to be as hard as he could so that I would never forget our last coming together. It was hard and fast with him furiously ramming himself up my backside as I revelled in this form of "rape" and loved the man for doing it. I cried when he kissed me goodbye and then he was gone and suddenly my life was once again empty.

I moped around all day, cleaning the flat and removing all traces of Eddie, though I didn't wash the sheets for they still had his smell and it was only this that comforted me as I went to sleep by myself for the first time for nearly four weeks.

It must have been about four o'clock in the morning when I was suddenly woken up by a massive hammering at my front door. I heard the words "Police" and guessed that they had been tipped off. I was glad that they were too late, and slowly got out of bed and went and stood by the open bedroom door as they broke down the outside door to the flat.

Two plain clothes policemen and six uniformed constables spilled into the flat and saw me standing there naked to face them.

'Where is he?' I was asked as three of the coppers surged forward to knock me aside as they went into the bedroom.

'Who?' I asked, giving them a bewildered look.

'Eddie Forbes! We know he's here.'

'Well he's not and this is the second time that you lot have been here looking for him,' I said, thanking my lucky stars that I'd cleaned every piece of china, the walls and everywhere that he could have possibly touched during his stay with me.

'Not here sir,' said one of the constables, pushing past me again as he emerged from the bedroom. The senior of the two plain clothes men snapped out.

'Get forensics over here to check this place out. You,' he said to me, 'Get dressed. You're coming with us.'

'Why?'

'For aiding and abetting an escaped felon and there's a good chance of hanging a murder rap round your neck at the same time,' he said.

'You're barking fucking mad!' I shouted back at him but I was pushed back into the bedroom.

'Just get dressed for you're coming with us,' he snarled. I think he was in a bad temper for not having found Eddie in the flat. I went to my wardrobe and got out a dress and then the dresser and put on stockings and belt before slipping the dress on and finally my shoes.

'Fer Christ's sake you fucking faggot! Why the dress?' he shouted at me.

'That's all the clothes I've got here,' I shouted back at him as I was then being hustled out by two of the coppers. 'You can't do this to me,' I almost screamed as I was bundled down the stairs and outside and shoved into the back of a police car. Then I had two get inside also, one on either side of me and the car took off like a rocket. I noticed from the route we'd taken that I was going to finish up in Bow Street.

I was hauled inside and formally charged with aiding and abetting an escaped felon and then taken down some stairs and shoved into a cell and had the door clang shut behind me and hear the sound of a heavy bolt being used to make sure I was secure inside.

I sat in that small cell fuming and running through my mind the progress I had made in the cleaning of my flat and kept wondering if I'd missed any fingerprints of Eddie. At least I was given breakfast, which made me laugh for it was porridge. It was after this that I began to bang on the door demanding my right to a phone call. After being told many times to shut up I was eventually let out and led to the end of the corridor where there was a phone and explained that I had to make two calls, one being to directory enquiries as I didn't know the number I wanted.

I did, but I just wanted as much time out of that cell as possible. I was given a number from my enquiry which I knew was no good and then phoned the number that I knew would get me through to Miss Winters.

'Miss Winters here, how may I help you?' was what I got when she answered the phone.

'Help me, please. It's infamy, infamy, they've all got it in for me!' I cried. Laughing to myself for I'd been able to quote that famous line of Kenneth Williams in the film, Carry On Cleo, where he plays the part of Caesar and knowing that he is being killed.

'They've just gone and arrested me on a wild trumped up charge,' I shouted down the phone.

'Is that you, Jackie?' came her voice.

'Yes. I'm being held in Bow Street. I don't know of anyone else who can help me, please, come and get me out.' I'd put a sob into my voice and with it now being a nice mellow tone, it really sounded plaintive and would tug at anyone's heartstrings.

'I'll be right over,' she replied, breaking the connection.

'I'm Spartacus!' I cried to my guard in a triumphant voice but I think the irony was lost on him as he took me back to my cell. So I sat there for another two hours before the door opened and in came Miss Winters.

'Oh, Felicity. Thank heavens you've come. I'm at my wit's end as to what they are saying about me,' I cried. 'It's lies, all lies. They say I've been hiding Eddie Forbes and it isn't true! I've been a good girl, I have!' Shades of My Fair Lady, I was quoting Eliza Doolittle now, but it had its effect.

'There, there Jackie, calm down. We'll get this sorted out,' she said trying to placate me and pushed me back down onto the bunk.

'Just because I've been put inside once, they think I'm a hardened criminal! It's just not fair.'

'We'll sort out this mess, don't worry.'

'Worry! They also said that I might even be tried for murder! Murder! Me! What else are they going to accuse me of?' and I buried my face into my hands and began to sob.

'Murder? Don't be silly, you're overwrought,' she said as she put her arm round my shoulder and gave me a hug. 'We'll sort this out. Who's your solicitor?'

'Solicitor?' I asked, raising up my tear stained face. 'How the hell can I afford a solicitor on unemployment benefit?'

'Of course, well we'll sort that out, now tell me what happened.'

So I related all that had happened that morning adding that because I hadn't been sleeping too well I had been taking sleeping tablets and so it was some time before I was fully awake and by that time they had broken down the front door of my flat. 'Who's going to pay for that? I can't afford it and the landlord's going to want it replaced,' I cried.

Overall, I did a good job and had her eating out of my hand by the time we'd finished our talk, but I then threw in the bit about the possible murder charge.

'Well I did hear a little about this. It appears that they found a man's body in the Thames and it's possible that he might have been the man that attacked you.'

'How could they come to that assumption? I never knew the man that knifed me let alone go out and kill him,' I said.

She had no answer to this and as she had promised, later that afternoon I had a solicitor and found out that I would be held until the forensic team had finished with my flat. So I spent the night there and in the morning was asked to go along with a police woman constable to identify a body to see if it had been the man that attacked me. I didn't want to but was advised that it would clear the air if it wasn't the man, so I went.

He'd been alive when I'd cut his prick off but he was as dead as a doornail now lying on this table for me to look at his pasty face. No, I had said. That wasn't the man and so that ended that little scenario and what with the forensic team coming up with a blank in respect of having Eddie's fingerprints in my flat, I was released.

I was driven home and was pleased to see that the Social Services had seen to having got my front door repaired, using the same lock so that I could enter. The first thing I did was to pour myself out a treble gin with very little tonic and thanked my lucky stars once again for getting out of another scrape. I didn't leave my flat for three days but just sat there and reviewed at what I had gone through over the past half year.

Going back a bit earlier, I deliberately killed another man by cutting off his prick and letting him bleed to death. I had been a bloody good singer and that had been taken away from me by this man that I had killed. I had got into a pub brawl and as a consequence of fighting off the coppers, finished up in prison for three months. There I put myself under the protection of one man and let him fuck me every day of my time inside and then when he escapes, harbour him. Being hounded by the police at the same time and only getting away with it by the skin of my teeth.

Why oh why was I being plagued by all these mishaps of which I wasn't an instigator, only just a bystander? I was now out of work and on the dole. I couldn't do what I had liked to do and that was sing. But it was also what I was losing out on that got me, namely having men wanting to fuck me which was my main reason for living. A male erect penis, throbbing and pulsating and quivering to be pushed up into my backside for me to revel in being fucked in this fashion. How in hell's name was I now going to be able to get a man or men to fuck me. I couldn't go out on the streets dressed as a woman for that would probably attract the men who were seeking real women and get roughed up again and maybe even worse.

I think I was pissed for the whole three days as I tried to work out my future and what to do to get all that I wanted. Read that as a big, rampant cock and money at the same time. The last person I could ask about this was Felicity Winters which only left my girl friend Sally or Bert and Daniel. It was sad to think that I then realised that I had very few friends because I suppose it was my own ego that told me that I didn't need anyone else and I could survive on my own. I was wrong!

So I ventured out and went to the pub and met up with Bert and Daniel and told them of my dilemma but only after having asked about Eddie. It appeared that he'd been able to leave the country on his forged passport but as to where, they didn't know. With respect to the man I had killed, nothing had come close to them and so it was a closed chapter as far as they were concerned. As to my problem, it was Daniel who came up with the answer. He went off and made a couple of phone calls and came back with the solution. It was either a hit or miss situation as far as he could see it so it would be up to me to sell myself to get this particular job that would be, and he sniggered, right up my alley.

I was to call up Samantha's Escort Agency for an appointment and as he'd already given my name, would be seen at a time suitable to both parties. I thanked him for this and he finished his beer and went off to leave me alone with Bert.

'Er. Jackie….' he began and I knew by the way he looked and had started to speak what he wanted and as I was at a loose end at the moment forestalled him from going further.

'Yes Bert, the answer is yes,' I said as I got up and went off to the ladies toilet with him a short distance behind me, though in the next couple of minutes he would be closer. Alone in there, I gave him a kiss and asked him if he wanted me to suck him or did he want to fuck me. He opted for the latter and so I bent over and gave him the pleasure of lifting the hem of my dress to reveal the pale cheeks of my bum that he was about to stick his cock up in between. He wasn't the best of lovers but any port in a storm and I loved to feel the hardness of a rampant cock once again sliding up my back passage to soothe my inner nerves. He held my hips firmly as he pushed himself inside me and I loved that intrusion into my body and gave myself up to the thrill of once again being fucked by a man. He loved it too, I presume, for he always wanted me and he really did his best to please me at the same time as he moved himself in and out of my arse as he fucked me. He grunted and groaned as he came in short sharp bursts while I jerked off, making sure I didn't come over the lower front of my dress this time as I shot my load under the sink as his came inside me. I loved that first spurt as it was one I could feel and it always triggered me off into coming and the rest of his was just icing on the cake, well, my insides really but you know what I mean.

It was the last fuck he had for a long time for he was nicked the following day after an abortive attempt to steal from a local bookmaker. He'd been recognised and they nabbed him that evening before he'd even had a chance to spend any of what he'd gotten from them. He went down for five years.

But that was later, for I'd made my phone call and had set up an interview with Samantha for the following day. I took care in having a good bath with scents and powdering myself afterwards, though not too much and dressing carefully and seeing that my make-up was perfect before I sallied forth to try and get onto her books.

'Hello,' said this bright woman who I put at about thirty years of age, as I walked into the agency's office at the appointed time. 'My name is Samantha and you must be Jackie Trent,' she said as she offered her hand, which I shook. 'Let's go into my office.'

I smiled at the girl behind the desk where we'd met and guessed that she was the secretary as I followed Samantha into a small cramped room that boasted only a desk, two chairs and a telephone apart from a filing cabinet against one wall and two photos on the opposite one. One was of a good looking man and the other of two children.

'My father and my two children,' she said, seeing that I had stopped to look at them. 'He helped me start this business.'

'He looks a nice man,' I said.

'Yes. In more ways than most. The other picture is of his grand-children.' I got the vibes from this statement that the husband wasn't to be mentioned and so didn't say any more but sat down in the chair that faced her small desk.

'Now before we go into any detail let me say this up front. We here provide a service in being an escort agency. We charge all our clients one hundred pounds an evening for the escort they have and that person receives seventy pounds for the five hours, that being seven in the evening till midnight.

'Now if the client wishes the company of the escort for longer after midnight,' she went on, 'that is up to the escort to dictate the terms. We have no knowledge of what goes on after this time and do not wish to know for we are not a brothel organisation. We just supply the escort. What happens afterwards is of no concern to us. Is this quite clear?'

'Yes,' I said.

'You have been favourably recommended by a good client and we will take that as read. Have you done this sort of thing before?'

'Well after a fashion. I've entertained many men in my time for I used to be a singer until an unfortunate occurrence which has since cur-tailed my singing career. I know how to behave when with a man and how far to go, if,' I added hastily, 'if he would wish to go further as you say after midnight.'

'Well you dress well and have beautiful eyes so I think you might do well with us. We have an extensive wardrobe in the next room for we record every dress worn when out with a client so that you never turn up on duty with one that you have been out with him before. Though we do charge ten pounds a night per dress to cover the wear, tear and cleaning. We currently have twelve females and three men on our books and are always looking out for more recruitments such as yourself because the demand is greater than our supply,' she finished with a smile. This I wiped off in no short order.

'But, ah, er, which category do you put me into?' I asked, giving her a sweet smile.

'With the women of course. You are rather beautiful and would in time be much in demand by our male clients,' she said.

'But would those men be happy enough to be going out with another man dressed as a woman?'

'I don't…..Oh My God!' she stammered out. 'You don't mean to say…….'

'Yes. I'm a transvestite, and before you blow a gasket, there are many men out there that would be proud to have me on their arm knowing that it is a man that they are with and to be able to….well, let's say, that is what would happen after midnight.'

'I…I…I just don't know what to say to this. No. It's outrageous, you coming in here posing as a woman and letting me believe you were one,' she spluttered.

'I'm very sorry if I've upset you for that was the least of my intentions. I've have just come here in good faith to ask to be employed as an escort, and believe me, there are many men out there in the world that would just love the charade of being out with a supposable female when they are then cocking a snoot at their friends by knowing exactly what's under this dress. If you, as female, and don't get me wrong in saying this, but if you can be fooled into believing that I'm a woman, think of how your male clients that I am offered to will respond. I can guarantee that I'll have as many requests once it is known that you also have people such as me on your books. You'll finish up hiring more of my type of person.' There! I'd made my spiel and the ball was now in her court though I still crossed my fingers.

Though I realised later that I could have set up my own escort agency that only supplied transvestites and would have made a lot of money but then I would have been out with the clients most of time and not seen to the office side of things.

'Well I don't know,' Samantha said pensively as she looked now very critically at me, 'but you certainly fooled me.'

'How do you answer the phone? Do you say after the title that you have men and women available for escort duties? Why not add, and male transvestites. Believe me, it might shock some but I think you'd be surprised at the response to the latter. To be rather blunt, there are many men out there that would like the opportunity to be able to satisfy a deep buried urge to have sex with a member of their own sex, especially if the person is dressed up as a woman.' Still she looked dubious and fiddled with a pen at the desk and I now crossed my legs as well in the hope that she would take the chance on me.

She did!

'Okay,' she said slowly, 'We'll give it a try but I don't hold out much hope. Give me all your details on this form and you will have to be examined by our doctor every six months, er, I think you can understand why?'

'Certainly,' I said. 'When can I start?'

'As soon as the doctor can say that you are, er, ah, clean. Er, this is part of the contract that you see him every six months, failure to do so results in you being taken off the books.'

'I understand that. Can you make me the appointment now?'

'The secretary will do that and if all is well, I'll, er, add what you suggested when I talk to my clients.'

With that, I was in, not expecting any problems with the doctor who the secretary fixed the appointment for that afternoon. Boy, was he in for a shock and he was when he saw me enter as a woman and when my dress was off to see a man.

'Oh, ah, er, well, I was expecting to examine a woman,' he said all of a fluster. 'Coming from the agency.'

'Don't you examine the men as well from there?' I asked.

'Yes, but they normally come wearing trousers or a suit, not in a dress,' he replied.

'So what do you examine? The body or the clothes?' I asked with a sweet smile.

'The body of course!'

'Well, here's the body. Just pass me fit and I can then start work.'

I was passed fit and clean of any discernable diseases and I went home and fretted. Would she add the rider that she also had a transvestite on her books or chicken out and not say a word and then tell me that nobody wanted me. I got pissed that night thinking that that would be the case and it would be another career move that failed. She had my mobile number and I made sure that it was fully charged, but it didn't ring.

I was in limbo. Oh why did this have to happen to me. Sally would have jumped at the chance of fucking me and I liked to think that Bambi would have too, but they were working in the club. Bert was back inside and after the remarks from Daniel, I don't think he would get his cock out for me. So I spent a miserable night alone again with the only solace left to me and that was my own right hand to give me relief and let me sleep.

All of the next day I fretted and literally pounced on the mobile phone when it rang to find that it was Samantha.

'I don't know if you're a witch or have some kind of magic but I have a client that is interested in having you as an escort, contrary to my expectations. Are you available tonight from seven o'clock?'

'Yes,' I said, my heart thumping inside my chest. 'Where and when?' She gave me all the details and so I got myself ready for the appointed time and went and met the man who wanted a transvestite as his date for the evening. The fact that he'd wanted someone like me told me that I was onto a winner.

What I didn't know then was that Samantha already had a transvestite on her books and the reason she had taken me on was because she had been getting enquiries about such as me and that the other person whose name was David, or was really known at the agency as Davinia. She had started about three months before me and wasn't able to cope with the demands that Samantha had been getting, so I was taken on to catch the overflow as it were. But back to my first escort job.

It was for a function at the Dorchester Hotel where he was staying and I had to meet him in the bar at seven o'clock. There were quite a few people in the bar and so I went up to the bar and asked the barman if he knew which gentleman was a Mr. Childers.

'Ah yes. He said he was expecting someone. He's the gentleman at the end.' I thanked him and moved down the bar.

'Mr. Childers?' I asked of the man indicated who looked to be about fifty years of age, greying slightly at the temples, clean shaven and wearing a rather expensive suit. His face was unremarkable except he had a nice smile and white teeth and his eyes crinkled up with the smile.

'Ah, Miss Trent, it's a pleasure to meet you,' he said offering me his hand. I shook it.

'It's a pleasure to meet you and the name is Jackie,' I said smiling back at him as his eyes moved up and down as if looking for a flaw.

'And mine's Robert, and I must say you look lovely.'

'Thank you sir,' giving him a short curtsey.

'What would you like to drink, the show doesn't start till eight?' I told him and he got that and another one for himself and led me over to a small table where we sat down.

'I've used Samantha's agency a few times but this was the first time that she said she had someone like you and it intrigued me and I must say that you have stunned me. You look flawless and really beautiful,' he said as he put his hand on mine, 'so much so that I'm not going to beat around the bush. Would you stay the night with me tonight?'

'I'm on escort duty till midnight,' I said, 'but after that, the time's my own.'

'Would you then, after midnight? I'll pay you two hundred pounds and throw in breakfast too.' Now that wasn't a bad offer for him to get what he wants, me to get what I want and get paid that much, well I couldn't refuse and accepted his offer. I had a six pack of condoms in my bag and hoped that we'd get to use half of them at least, he looked capable enough.

We had another drink and made small talk until it was time for dinner and we went into one of the banqueting halls where there must have been at least three hundred people milling about finding seats at the numerous tables there. We sat down at one and introductions were made and we had an excellent meal and when the coffee was being served, the speeches began. This was the boring bit of how the industry had flourished over the past year and then came some awards and I was getting fidgety and Robert noticed this and whispered in my ear that he was bored too and would I like to go up to his room instead of waiting till all this finished. I looked at his wristwatch.

'But it's only eleven o'clock,' I whispered back.

'I'll add another fifty if we go now,' he whispered back.

Well I was all for that and said to him out loud that I was getting a headache, which gave him the excuse to make our apologies to the others at the table and he pulled out the chair for me and we said good night and left the hall.

He took my hand as we waited for the lift and he held it right up to the door of his room and only let go so that he could unlock the door. He ushered me inside and shut the door behind him and only turned on the bathroom light, which left the main part of the room in shadow but still with enough light for us to see each other.

He pulled me into his arms and kissed me with his mouth open. Feeling his tongue push forward, I opened mine too, then sucked on his tongue and let him suck on mine as we stood with our mouths glued to each other. His body was pressing up against mine and I could feel that he was hard and began to undo his belt first and slipped my hand inside and grasped his erection. He gave out a groan as my fingers curled round it and quickly released me to take off his jacket and tie while I still held onto him. His shirt was soon off and I pulled his trousers down to free his throbbing piece of meat and went down onto my knees and took him into my mouth and gave him a few chews before sucking and licking the head of his cock.

'Not too much Jackie,' he said in a hoarse voice as he pulled himself back out. He got his feet free from his trousers and looked at me as I hadn't as yet moved. 'Oh, yes, of course,' he stammered and went to his jacket and pulled out his wallet and counted out two hundred and fifty pounds and gave it to me. I thanked him and put the money in my bag and then took off my dress as he sat down on the edge of the bed to watch me.

I had turned so that he saw my back first, black bra, black stocking held up by the same coloured suspender belt, the cheeks of my bum being framed by these accessories.

'I can't tell from this angle for you have the waist, hips and legs of a female,' he said and I looked over my shoulder at him and smiled and then turned round for him to see that I was indeed a male and had an erection to prove it.

'Lovely,' he breathed, 'Absolutely lovely.'

His eyes were gleaming as he beckoned me closer and when close enough, took hold of my cock and gave it a rub before taking me into his mouth. I didn't stop him as he had to me but held his head in between my hands and let him carry on as I gently face fucked him, coming in his mouth which he swallowed with ease. He hadn't bothered to hold the base of my prick whilst he was sucking but kept on rubbing his hands up and down the cheeks of my bum. It had been a long time for me since I'd had another man suck on my cock and take it all down. It certainly relieved the ache in my balls.

'Now it's my turn,' he said. 'I've been thinking about this ever since I phoned the agency.'

I went and got the condoms out of my bag and quickly unwrapped one and went down onto my knees and gave his trembling cock a kiss and a quick suck before rolling the condom down over the head and down the shaft. I also had a tube of cream in my bag just in case I met one of those monster men but as Robert was of an average size in that department, I didn't need any.

I got onto the bed and went into my favourite position. On my knees and leaning forward on my elbows so that I could lay the side of my face on the covers. By getting as much of my upper chest on the bed and bending my body downwards, made my arse stick right up in the air. This was an invitation to any erect cock and I felt the bed move as Robert got on and had his hands run once again over the cheeks of my bum before I felt the head of his prick probe the entrance to my cave.

It was lovely to have the head widen me enough for it to slip inside and then feel it pass the portals and be followed by the thickening shaft to fill the void within me.

'That's just great Robert,' I said with a gasp which was for his benefit for I took him in quite easily, as his thighs pressed up to my bum. I felt his cock throbbing and waited for him to begin and start to scratch the itch I now had inside and gave out a gurgle as he began to move and fuck me. How glorious it was to have a cock once again reaming me and giving me as much pleasure as the owner was getting from doing so.

But like all men, he didn't last two minutes before he was gripping my hips hard and battering away at my backside in short sharp jerks as he came.

'That was nice and tight,' he said panting when he came to a full stop, his cock still pulsating inside me and then I gave out that little cry when he pulled out. I quickly turned round and pulled off the condom and took his still wet and hard cock into my mouth to suck out the residue of his sperm. I think he liked this extra touch and stroked my hair as I sucked on him.

'That was really great,' he said after he'd flopped down onto the bed, lying on his back. I moved into his arms and told him that he had the strength of a young man, which pleased him, and begged him to rise up soon and have me again. This took over an hour of me sucking and playing with his balls as well as his limp dick. I certainly worked hard for the money I had been paid.

It was well over an hour before, like Lazarus, he rose up from the dead and fucked me again, lasting nearly twice as long this time. Instead of him going down on me this time, he stayed with his cock up my arse and jerked me off, making my load shoot out onto the bed covers.

After the cleaning up process, we got into bed properly for me to cuddle up to him and we drifted off to sleep. He fucked me again in the morning and while I had a shower, he ordered breakfast to be sent up to the room. I only put on my underwear to sit down and eat which I think pleased him and after the meal, put on my dress, gave him a kiss and thanked him for such a wonderful night. I also got him to promise to ring the agency the next time he was down in London so that we could have a repeat performance.

I took a taxi home, well satisfied with what I'd been paid and having had a cock at the same time and couldn't wait for my next job. Meanwhile, I went and signed off from the employment exchange and waited at home for the phone to ring. It was three days before I got the call from Samantha and this, as I found out later, was because Davinia had already been booked out. It was two months before I learned of her existence but there weren't any sour grapes because she had been there first and clients had got round to asking for her by name, as they did with me after they'd once had the chance to fuck me.

I had a nice surprise one morning to find that I'd received a postcard. All that was written on it was my name and address so it could only have been from Eddie and it had a Spanish stamp on it. On the other side it had four small pictures with the word Murcia in the middle. They were different scenes being Mazarron, Bolneuvo, Porte de Mazarron and La Azohia. This last name had a faint line drawn underneath it which told me where he was though I had to look the places up in my atlas to find them. This only showed Mazarron but the other places must have been quite near to this town. It was nice to know that he was now somewhere safe.

***

So after three months of being with the agency, I was going out and being treated to dinner and fucked nearly every night of the week. It was around this time that I eventually bumped into Davinia in the agency wardrobe where we were both looking for a dress to wear for our night's date. We introduced ourselves and had a laugh for she had taken me for a real woman though I'm pleased to say that I knew it was her straight away. She just didn't have the aplomb that I had acquired over the years and wasn't as good looking as me. We also laughed when we discussed the clients we'd been out with and found that we had quite often shared the same one, though I'm pleased to say I had more of her leftovers than she had of mine.

I also met some of the others that were employed by Samantha. There was Ralph, a big, young black man. He was every inch the perfect gentleman and was always requested but, he admitted sadly, always by women that were twice his age and nowhere as good looking as me.

Violet was a good laugh, a very effervescent young girl that also was in great demand but had to take second place to Magenta, another young thing that even I envied for the luxuriant head of hair that went with her name. She eventually got married and became Lady Bentley, but still continued to work on at the agency.

It was whispered that her husband was a confirmed homosexual. *(Ed. Read the books Lady Magenta, Lady of Pleasure, and Lady of Cuckolds for her story.)*

My twenty-first birthday was fast approaching and I got Sally to agree to take the night off and spend the day celebrating with me for I'd already told Samantha well in advance that I wouldn't be available that night. We didn't celebrate it as I had planned for I received a phone call four days before the event.

'Mr. Trent?' the male voice asked.

'No. It's Miss Trent. Jackie Trent,' I replied. 'Who's calling?'

'You don't know me but I'm the vicar of your home village. I've bad news, I'm afraid. Your Aunt Julia passed away in her sleep the day before yesterday.'

'Oh dear God,' I said, tears springing to my eyes.

'She's with him now. She didn't suffer. She knew she was going and because of this I would look in every day. I'm sorry to break this news over the phone but we've only just found your telephone number among her papers. That is, me and her solicitor.'

'I'd better come down to make the arrangements,' I said, not seeing my reflection in the mirror in the hall where my phone was, for the tears blurring my eyes. I'm sure he could tell that I was crying.

'There's no need to rush down here for everything is in hand. She herself had already made arrangements with the undertakers and the funeral will take place on Wednesday.'

My birthday!

'Can't you change the date?' I asked.

'No. Everything has been set in motion and the people of the village have been told.'

'Okay,' I said dully, 'I'll be down there that morning. Thank you for letting me know.'

What a happy birthday that was going to be, burying your aunt on the very day you reach twenty-one. I phoned Sally when I was more composed and she gave me her condolences and said that she wouldn't let me down and would come with me to the funeral and then we could spend the night somewhere to celebrate my belated birthday. Which I read to mean that she would fuck me as much as she could in appeasement. Well I expected it anyway, but didn't say this as I thanked her.

I went out and bought a black dress that was suitable for the funeral but one that could also be used for my agency work too. Do you know that for the life of me I cannot remember the next three men I went out with on my escort duties. I know I was nicely fucked by all three, but how, where and what else we did, I just cannot bring those men up in my mind.

I was late getting home, well, the early hours of the morning and went to bed and when I woke up wished myself a happy but miserable birthday. I'd never felt so down in my life, except when I had finally realised I'd been knifed in the throat and couldn't sing anymore. That was how low I felt on that morning which should have been one of my happiest. I wasn't even dressed when Sally called round and she only had coffee while I picked at the breakfast I'd made for myself. I then had my shower and got dressed and unconsciously dressed as I normally did in my underwear and dress.

'Don't they know you as a man?' she asked me and I looked at her dressed as I was, in female attire.

'I'll tell them that I was always a tomboy as they knew me but I was really a girl. What about you?'

'No one's going to pay any attention to me, besides, I've changed quite a bit since we left the village. They won't remember me, but with you it will be different.'

'Well I've got an answer for that,' I said, an excuse which I found I had to use later in the day.

We left my flat and took a taxi to the station and then another local taxi when we arrived to take us to my late aunt's home. It brought back both happy and sad memories, the most predominate of the latter being my uncle's death. It had been hard on my aunt but years after his passing, she had come back to life. She was gone for good now though, and the place seemed strange without her around.

The timing had been right for the vicar was there to meet us and gave us a glass of sherry before it was time to go to the church for the service. There were about forty of us in the church and the service was quickly over and we trooped out, following the coffin and watched it being lowered into the ground with me throwing in the first handful of dirt.

The vicar, lovely man, had also seen to having some eats and drinks for those that had attended and though I got some curious looks from the others, no one had to guts to come out with what they might have been thinking at seeing me in a dress. As Sally had predicted, nobody took any notice of her the whole time.

It was with some relief when the last mourner had left leaving just me, Sally, the vicar and the solicitor whose name I didn't catch. But it was him who changed my life.

'Ah, now that all that had to be done is done,' he began and I thought, what a prick. 'Let's sit down so that I can read your late aunt's will.'

This we duly did, sitting round the dining room table that was still littered with the aftermath of the funeral repast. He cleared a space and brought some papers out of a briefcase he had brought with him.

'We are gathered here together today,' he began. 'Oh, sorry vicar,' he said with a little laugh. 'It's words that you normally use for something quite different, please accept my apologies.' He cleared his throat and started again. 'I'm here to read the will of your late aunt Julia, though I was led to believe that you were a, er, male, because you are named as Jack Trent.' He looked at me through the spectacles perched on the end of his nose.

'For that, you can blame both my father and the register clerk, for my dad was half pissed and the clerk was half deaf. The clerk thought he heard the word Jack and wrote that down and assumed that it was a male child he was registering. Dad was too far gone to notice the mistake for he had said that my name was Jackie, but I am one and the same, if you follow me?'

'Yes, yes, quite. Well, without going through all the words written here in the will of your aunt, you are to inherit the house and grounds and all other assets that she owned. These latter are in shares and trusts plus what was in the bank which total about a quarter of a million pounds. The value of the house hasn't yet been verified.'

Hap, hap, happy birthday! my mind cried out as I took this in. The house and all that money made me a millionaire! I gasped and turned to Sally, who had also gasped and her face was creased in a smile as we hugged each other much to the amusement of the other two.

'Oh, I've just realised the date,' the solicitor said. 'Belated birthday wishes are in order,' to which the vicar added his. 'This most certainly will be a day for you to remember,' he added. 'Just a word of caution. Just think carefully before you act on what you will do with your inheritance. My door will always be open if you wish to seek my advice.'

'Thank you,' I said, 'I'll do that. We were planning on going back to London tonight, but I think in the circumstances, we'll stay over and go back tomorrow. Is it possible to have the keys?'

'By all means,' he said, passing them over. 'It would help me if you could call into the office in the morning and sign a few things to keep the paperwork correct.' This I agreed to do and on thanking him and the vicar, they both left and Sally and I then hugged each other again.

'Well Miss Rich Bitch, what are your plans now?' she asked me.

'I'd like to go to bed so that you can fuck me to prove that I'm not dreaming,' I said, giving her a kiss.

'Good idea, and then you can fuck me.'

We went upstairs to my old room and there we undressed and went to bed and said bugger to the use of condoms and fucked each other silly.

'So are you going to give up work and stay down here then?' Sally asked as we lay together, dressed only in our underwear on the bed.

'I'm not burying myself away here without a rampant cock to service me every night. No, I think I'll get a small place of my own in London somewhere and carry on at the agency. Now don't tell them a word,' I said, sitting up and leaning over her. 'They're not to know that I've come into some money. It could cause some problems.'

'I won't breathe a word. Can you lend me a couple of thousand?' she smiled.

'That's what I mean,' I said as I gave her a friendly slap, 'but for you, yes, but no one else. Now that's raised your little bugger up,' I said as I stroked her erection. 'Show me how much you love me with it.'

I turned over and went onto my knees and had the pleasure of having Sally's cock slide up into me and give me a wonderful fuck. After I had pleasured her too, we went and washed and got dressed and explored the house.

There was quite a lot of antique furniture which wasn't my style and if I bought myself a small place it wouldn't fit so I decided to come down the next week and pick out what I wanted to keep and have the rest shipped off to auction.

We also found enough food and drink for us to cook my birthday dinner for Sally didn't want to go down to village to eat in case she was recognised. So just the two of us celebrated my birthday and got quite rat arsed and went to bed and still managed to fuck one another again before falling asleep in the same bed.

It was surprising that we didn't have hangovers the next day and on the way to the station, we stopped off at the solicitor's and I signed what papers he wanted done and told him that I would be down in about a week's time to tell him what I would be doing in respect of the house and its contents.

Sally and I duly got the train to London and I got a taxi to drop her off at her place before going on to mine. It was only on entering what was my place that I realised how seedy and rundown the whole bloody building was and it confirmed my resolve to start house hunting soon. I was disappointed that I hadn't been called by the agency and so I went to bed early but got a call the next morning. I was quite happy at that and got the client I escorted to ask me to stay the night and enjoyed sucking on his cock and having him fuck me.

Over the next week I went and looked at houses, not liking any of them really and also called in at some auctioneers that would only be too happy to sell what I offered. I decided to stay down at the house for a few days. One to select what I wanted to be collected for myself and put into storage for the time being and then have the rest collected by the selected auction house. Sally couldn't get the time off and I told Samantha that I wouldn't be available for those three nights and so went down on my own.

I spent the whole day labelling what I would keep and the following day, the van turned up to collect and take them for storage. The next day, two pantechnicons arrived to clear the rest of the house and when this was finally completed, I went to the solicitor and told him to put the house on the market. Having already spoken to two estate agents, it was agreed that the asking price would be one and a half million pounds. Considering the size of the house and surrounding grounds, it was a good price. To finish this little bit off, it was sold a month later after refusing to drop the price, it still went at what I had asked. This money was duly lodged in my bank in London after all the papers had been signed and I was now ready to buy my own place and get out of what I had now come to consider the hovel I'd been living in.

The house I settled on was just off the King's Road in Chelsea and it cost just over half a million pounds and would need several thousands to bring it up to scratch. So it was another two months before it was ready for me to move into and I was really glad to leave my old place and have a decent place to now call home. One other thing to the good was that I was now only a short walk away from where Samantha had the agency.

I had an encounter one day as I walked down the King's Road, arms loaded with shopping when I stepped off the curb and trod on a small piece of wood and started to stumble forward into the road when a man caught my arm and hauled me upright, preventing me from falling flat on my face.

'Are you alright?' he asked anxiously, feeling me trembling all over. He was clean shaven, had black hair and I put his age at about forty. His eyes were bright and he had a nice smile that I saw afterwards. 'It's lucky I was there waiting to cross the road.'

'Yes thank you,' I stuttered, instantly liking this man as I now saw his smile at me being okay. I didn't object to his taking my arm and seeing me safely across the road and I thanked him again and we went off in opposite directions. I was to meet him again in a few days' time.

I was now out five or six evenings a week on escort duty and I loved every minute of it. Being feted as it were at dinners and the like and then getting the inevitable proposal that I spend the night with them. With clients specifically asking for Davinia and myself, it was obvious that they preferred to fuck a man than a woman, so I was always asked and I never turned down one chance of sucking on a cock and also have it used up my backside.

'It's a dinner and dance at the Cumberland Hotel,' Samantha told me over the phone. 'Seven o'clock and his name is Doctor Forrester. You're to go straight in and up to his room where he'll meet you. Room three-oh-six.'

So I had a lovely scented bath in my new home and dressed carefully and made sure my make-up was perfect and rang for a taxi to take me to the Cumberland just before seven. I'd been to this hotel twice before and so knew the layout and walked straight through the lobby area and over to the lifts. I knocked at the door and got a nice surprise when it opened, for there was the man that had prevented me from the fall in the King's Road.

'You!' he exclaimed when he saw me and I nodded with a smile as big as his was. 'Well I never,' he said as he stood to one side to let me enter his room. 'You…your…a, well, the other day I wouldn't have thought it. You looked so perfect! Just as you do now and it's astounded me.'

'Me too that we should meet up again like this,' I said as I went and sat down on the bed. 'Do I get offered a drink?' I asked.

'Oh, of course, sorry,' he apologised as he seemed to unglue himself from by the door, which he now shut and moved over to the mini bar. 'It's just seeing you again and knowing that….that,' he stammered to a halt.

'I'm a man dressed as a woman. A transvestite,' I supplied for him to nod. 'A gin and tonic please,' I asked as he stood by the open fridge door.

'Ah yes. I never even thought of you this way the other day. You seemed so poised, so assured, so…so feminine.' I thanked him for the drink that he passed to me.

'Was that why you didn't make a pass at me?' I asked coyly, looking at him over the rim of my glass and had the pleasure of seeing him blush.

'Yes,' he said, looking down at his own glass.

'Well we both know now where we stand. Do I take it that you still want me……for escort duty?' I asked with a smile having staggered my words for him to get the message. He obviously did.

'Oh definitely. It's a reunion that the university holds every five years. Being a single man, I was plagued by women with marriageable daughters or unmarried sisters last time, which is not my scene. That's why I wanted an escort tonight to prevent the same happening again this year.'

'But you wanted a transvestite. So that it would look as though you were already fixed up.'

'Yes, that's it exactly,' he said with some relief on his face.

'But you are really a homosexual who won't come out of the closet, like me?' I said softly. He looked down at his glass again and nodded his head.

'I can't because of my position. I'm a practising doctor and it would do great harm to my career.'

'Well doctor, I think we are going to get along just fine,' I said finishing my drink and passing him the empty glass. 'My name's Jackie.'

'Mine's Julian,' he said with a happy smile on his face as he took my glass. 'Shall we go and have a ball?'

'One now and two later?' I asked with another smile.

'You're not backward about coming forward are you,' he said with a laugh as he took my arm and we went out of his room and down to the ballroom.

I think he took great pleasure in introducing me to other people, especially the women who had other young things alongside them. We had an excellent meal and I danced quite a few with him and also with some of the other men that were at our table. There must have been over four hundred people there at the beginning but by the time they played the last waltz, half of them had already disappeared.

It was heaven to be in his arms as we danced this last one and I wasn't surprised when he whispered in my ear.

'Will you stay the night with me?'

'One ball coming to an end and another two to go,' I said, 'and the answer's yes, if you've got what's normally attached to them.' To prove he did, he pulled me tighter to him so that I could feel that he certainly did have what I wanted.

The dance ended and he kissed me rather deeply right there in the middle of the dance floor and I couldn't but help get an erection myself and had to keep my hands together over my front as we returned to our table for me to collect my bag. Goodnights were said and he took my arm and led me out and back up to his room.

'Oh Jackie,' he said as soon as the door had closed behind us as he took me into his arms and kissed me. 'You were absolutely wonderful tonight. Didn't you see the green eyes of jealousy from the other young women there?'

'Yes,' I said, returning his kiss, 'I just hope that I'm going to get what they wanted.' I'd already started to unbutton his shirt and now he was quickly starting to take the rest of his clothes off and he had a lovely big erection sticking out in front of him.

'Just what the doctor ordered,' I said as I went down onto my knees and took the head of his throbbing cock into my mouth. 'Mmmmm,' I mouthed round the head as I sucked on him.

'Not yet,' he begged as he pulled himself out and helped me up from the floor where he lifted up my dress and pulled it over my head. This I shook to free my hair that fell back into its perfect shape by framing my face. 'Oh God,' he stammered as he looked at me standing there in female underwear with an erection jutting out from my pubic hairs. He then did the same as me by falling down onto his knees and taking me into his hot mouth. I think he was more sex-starved than I was the way he sucked, tongued and tried to chew it off.

'No Julian,' I cried, pulling back the same way. 'I want you to fuck me. If you use a condom I can then suck you afterwards.' I went and got onto the bed as he went to his open suitcase and pulled out a box of the things and quickly pulled one out and tore the wrapper off and rolled it down over his swaying cock.

'Cream or milk?' he joked as he got on the bed behind me.

'I'll take it as it comes,' I said, my voice muffled by the bedcovers for I was right down with my arse high in the air, the suspender straps straining.

'Coming straight up,' he said as his hand held my hip and I felt the head of his cock nuzzle my back passage and he pushed forward and I had the pleasure of a little pain as he widened me enough to enter and then the whole length of him slid inside me.

I gurgled with delight and gave his cock a squeeze with my sphincter muscle as he settled himself down to roger me. It was lovely to have a cock as big as his moving inside me, setting all my nerves atingle and lighting the fire within. He even began crooning as he fucked me with his slow in and out movements that was sheer bliss for me and really liked his grasping of me tight to ram himself tight up to my bum as he began to shoot his load. Jerking away and having his balls slap me as they swung back and forth as they began to lose the contents that had been fermenting inside.

As much as I hated him pulling out of me, I couldn't wait to turn round and whip off the condom to take the sperm coated head of his piece into my mouth to suck out what was left in the tube, to taste and savour his seed. It was lovely as I sucked and fondled his balls at the same time trying to ignore my own throbbing cock that was also begging for release.

Then it was my turn and I looked down at his strong lithe body that was bloody good and strong for man of his age. Moderately tanned with his bum so white and his solid thighs. I teased him with the head of my prick at the entrance to his backside.

'Please Jackie,' he begged when he could take no more. 'Now. I want you now.' So I pushed and entered him and he gave out a big sigh as

I filled him and brought my thighs right up tight to the cheeks of his back-side. I then leaned over his back as far as I could and put my hands under-neath and raked my fingernails down over his chest, making sure that I caught his nipples in the process. 'Oh my God,' he spluttered and I felt his whole body tremble at what I was doing and he gave several more shud-ders as I also raked his waist before I began to move and fuck him.

I had long since learned the art of holding myself back and so I was able to move my cock in and out of him for nearly five minutes before starting to come. I then rammed into him and butted his butt quite a few times as I came, punching out my sperm into the condom up his arse and loved every minute of fucking this doctor who was mine for the night.

He too gave out a cry when I pulled out of him and he was quickly round as I had been and tore off the condom to suck on me.

'Jackie. That was just great,' he said between kisses as we held each other now that we'd finished.

'I was going to say the same thing,' I replied, kissing him just as fiercely, rubbing my body up against his. 'I can't wait for you to rise up again to have me.'

We lay there kissing and stroking each other and his hand was pushing its way through my hair and caressing my neck when I felt his fingers touch the scar there.

'What's this?' He said as he moved and came up on his elbow, pushing me down onto my back as his hand moved my hair to one side for him to see what he was touching. 'It's not a tracheotomy. It's in the wrong place. What was it?' There was a look of concern on his face as he asked me this.

'I was knifed outside of the club where I used to sing,' I said, tears coming to my eyes.

'Oh my dear, you poor thing. Yes, I remember reading about this young singer getting knifed but the name didn't register. It was you, then?'

'Yes,' I said, tears now beginning to roll down my cheeks. 'It put paid to my singing career.'

'But you've got such a beautiful, husky melodic voice. It puts me in mind of Joan Greenwood and Eartha Kitt. They both had a speaking voice similar to yours and what do you mean about it ending your singing career?'

'That's what the doctor told me. They operated twice on me to stitch me back up inside.'

'Well I won't say yes or no to that until I've had a look inside,' he said.

'What?' I asked, not sure if I'd heard him right.

'I'm in E.N.T,' he replied.

'What's that?' I asked.

'Ear, nose and throat. That's what I specialise in as a doctor. What hospital were you treated at?' I told him and he said that tomorrow we would both go there for him to check it all out. I asked him what he meant and he explained that after seeing all the notes, he would like to put me out and do an exploratory of my throat and larynx with a camera to see if there was anything he could do. I scoffed at the idea but he went on to explain that it was something he did for a living and a good one at that, he added. If he should find anything wrong, he would be able to put it right for me.

He spoke with such assurance that I agreed to do as he asked but this got taken over by what I had in my hand and that took precedent over all else and so I had him fuck me again. It was another pleasurably seeing to and I reciprocated by giving him, using his words, the best fucking session he'd ever had.

We woke up early in the morning and I turned round on the bed and took him into my mouth for oral sex with that hard-as-iron bar of a cock he had whilst he did the same to me. It was a lovely coming together, really getting a taste for him now, well more than a taste, a whole mouthful, which slithered down my throat like a linctus.

He ordered breakfast for two and we both had a shower and was dressed by the time it was delivered and after we'd eaten, he took me off to the hospital where I had been operated on. Well it was there that they held my notes and being the doctor he was, was soon able to get his hands on them. He took quite some time studying both the notes of the operations and of those from the aftercare as well as looking intently at the x-rays. He then excused himself and was gone for nearly an hour before returning.

I wanted to know what he thought and why had he been gone so long, but he wouldn't tell me as he took my arm and led me out of the hospital and hailed a taxi. He had it take us back to the Cumberland and then into the dining room and ordered a steak for himself and a light salad for me. Oh, he also allowed me to have one drink for that would be my last until tomorrow afternoon, he said.

'Why?' I asked.

'Because my sweet,' he began as he took my hand across the table. 'I've been inside you and now I'm going to have a look.'

'Up my arse?' I asked in a fierce whisper, not daring to say it out loud.

'I'm not a proctologist,' he laughed. 'No, tomorrow I've booked a theatre to put a camera down through those sweet lips and see if there's any lasting damage done to your throat.'

'I'd rather have your cock there,' I said with a shaky laugh.

'We'll use that too, first though. We'll have to be up early in the morning,' he said.

'Well we were both up quite early this morning,' I said.

'I meant getting out of bed, you minx,' he laughed.

'Now that we've eaten, can we go to bed and practice at getting up?' I enquired with a smile.

'I don't think we need much practice at that,' he laughed but must have liked the suggestion for he quickly called over the waiter and signed the bill and within fifteen minutes we were indeed up and began a lovely afternoon of fucking each other.

It carried on through the evening and on into the night as we fucked ourselves silly until nothing could have raised us and I felt myself falling in love with this wonderful doctor. I cried out when I was woken up with it still being dark outside, thinking that the hotel was on fire or something.

'Just a sip of water,' he told me after saying that he had the operating theatre from half past five that morning. Neither of us had breakfast and we were soon in a taxi and it didn't take long to get to the hospital at that time of the day. Before I knew it, I was on a gurney after being undressed and I had needles shoved in my arm and soon went out like a light. While I was being prepped, he was scrubbing up and was waiting for me when I was wheeled in and it wasn't long before he had this camera tube down into my throat and looked at the monitor to see what it showed. He told me later that it was there for just over five minutes while he looked and turned this way and that for it was all being taped for him to study later. The camera tube was pulled out and a gel pushed down to soothe my throat though it was sore for a couple of days afterwards.

I was given a throat gargle after I was fully awake and he thanked the nurses and sister as they dressed me, ignoring the strange looks he'd gotten from my being dressed the way I was when they all knew that I was a male. But being the doctor and surgeon that he was, they didn't dare give voice to their thoughts and I, in retrospect, think that he must at that point had some feelings of love towards me to go through with this, me being dressed as I was.

He took me back to the hotel and ordered from room service some consommé soup and soft bread and he hand fed me by dipping the bread in the soup till it was all soggy and easy for me to swallow. I found out later that he had resigned the register downstairs by adding my name as Mrs. Forrester saying that I had unexpectedly joined him. He fed me scrambled eggs for lunch and told me that he couldn't find fault with the operations that I had undergone but pooh-poohed the idea that I couldn't sing anymore.

'It's just that you need some special training to be able to use the voice you now have. It will seem strange at first but I guarantee that you will be singing before long, though in a lower key. In fact, it will I predict, be quite sexy and I can't wait to hear it. Though let's take it easy to begin with.'

'You really want to hear me sing?' I asked, sitting up in bed. I was still wearing my underwear for he liked seeing me wearing these female garments.

'Yes,' he said, taking hold of my hand. 'I want to hear you do what you've been told that you cannot do.'

'But that might take ages,' I cried.

'I'm happy to wait as long as necessary,' he said with a smile, squeezing my hand and I knew then that he was indeed falling in love with me as I was with him.

'What about the hospital? Who's paying for that?'

'Did you ask me for any money when you agreed to sleep with me?' he asked.

'No, but.....'

'No buts. It's all been sorted so don't worry about a thing. You helped me and I've helped you so let's say no more on the subject.'

'Oh, I'd better phone the agency to let them know that I'm not available for the moment,' I said.

'I've already done that,' he answered. 'I told Samantha that you've undergone some minor throat surgery and will be out of action for a while. I'm going to look after you.'

'Oh Julian,' I said, tears springing to my eyes.

'There, there,' he said in a soothing voice. 'Now we'll leave your throat to get better. But how about we now inspect the other end?' he asked with a gleam in his eye.

'Is it what the doctor recommends?' I asked, smiling through my tears.

'It's what the doctor's ordered!' he said in a stern voice but spoken with a smile.

'Will your examination help to relax me?'

'A smooth internal massage might be the answer.'

'Do you have the right tool for this examination and massage?'

'One I always have with me for this purpose,' he smiled.

'Then let's use this tool of yours for the examination and internal massage and hope that it will indeed relax me,' I said as I turned over on the bed and waited for him to get behind me. I heard the rustle of his clothes as he took them off and felt the bed dip as he got on and had a shock as I felt his finger being pushed up into my behind.

'What's that?' I cried, giving a little jump at the sudden small intrusion.

'Just a minor probe to see if your reflexes are okay, which I'm pleased to say that they are,' he laughed.

'Well use your tool now for the massage for I cannot wait to be relaxed,' I said.

He did, and I drooled as I felt his cock enter me and slide right in and begin to give me that internal massage.

'I think I'm coming to love you, Julian,' I said under my breath.

'I'm coming to love you too,' he replied and it jolted me that he'd heard what I'd almost whispered. 'I am also coming at the same time.' He carried on as his movements became faster and he moved his cock in and out of me before grasping my hips tight and really pumping himself hard up against my rear as he shot his load inside me. My erection was hurting me and I squeezed him with my inside muscle.

'Stay there Julian,' I gasped as I began to ease myself down onto the bedcovers, squashing my penis. 'Now ride me as you are.'

He began to move whilst laying on my back and his body movement was moving me and was making me fuck the bed. I loved his weight on me and begged him to move faster and harder. This he did and I began to groan and then had my release, squishing out my sperm between my stomach and the bed. I gave out a big sigh as I came.

'I've finished now,' I said, him knowing exactly what I'd done and he slowly pulled out of me as he went back up onto his knees. I rolled over out of the sticky mess I'd made and pulled off his condom and turned round on the bed so that we could both suck on each other to finish off the session. I couldn't do it as well as I normally did for my throat was still sore but it was enough to satisfy him at cleaning the mess off of the head of my cock.

The top cover of the bed had to be taken off because there was no way we could clean that properly and so we laid on the top sheet and kissed and stroked each other.

'Throat still sore?' he asked as we petted.

'A little but I think I'll be able to eat properly at dinner. But then we can't go down to the dining room for that,' I said.

'Why?' he asked.

'Well people saw me last night in my ball gown as well as when we came back from the hospital and I can't very well go downstairs again wearing the same dress. I'll have to ring Sally up to bring me something different to wear.'

'Nonsense,' he snorted and sat up and reached for the phone. 'This is Doctor Forrester, room three-oh-six. Can you put me through to the dress shop? Yes, thank you.' He waited for a moment and then repeated his name and room number. 'Hello. We have a problem here. My wife has mislaid her luggage and needs a dress to change into.' Wife? I looked at him and mouthed the word. He just shook his head and put a finger to his lips. 'Size? Oh, just a moment. What size dresses do you wear dear?' he asked me. I told him my size and he repeated it down the phone. 'Bring up three and we'll select one of them. Yes. Yes. Thank you very much.' He put the phone down and gave me a smile.

'What's with the wife bit?' I asked him.

'Well I couldn't keep ordering food for two and so I went down and told them that my wife had turned up unexpectedly and I booked you in as Mrs. Forrester. Anything wrong in that?' he asked with a smile.

'No,' I smiled back at him as I gave myself a stretch. 'Mrs. Jackie Forrester,' I murmured. 'I like the sound of that.'

'Well, Mrs. Forrester, I suggest you put on your underwear and cover yourself up with a bath robe for the dresses will be here in a minute,' he said and gave my bum a light smack as I got off the bed and began to get dressed. I then put on a big white fluffy robe and was ready when the knock came at the door and he let in a middle-aged woman carrying three dresses draped over her arm.

'These are the best we have downstairs sir and all of the same size,' she said as she laid them out separately on the bed. They were lovely and I picked the one that looked the best and held it up against me.

'Try it on, darling,' he said with an amused smile on his face. I think I went a bit red but because of that suggestion that I did so with her still in the room and so boldly turned my back on both of them so that they could only see the back view of me in my underwear and quickly slipped it over my head and snuggled it down over my hips and smoothed it out with my hands before I turned round to face them.

'Perfect,' he said. 'Any dress on you, dear, looks wonderful. Put the charge on my bill,' he said to the woman who smiled and picked up the other two dresses and left.

'Oh you darling man,' I said as I went into his arms and gave him a good kiss. 'Thank you for the dress, it's lovely.'

So with a new dress on, I was able to go down to dinner with him, though he only ordered what he knew I would be able to swallow without hurting my throat. Even though my meal was delicious I would still like to have eaten his porterhouse steak.

I thanked him again in bed that night by sitting on top of him and bouncing myself up and down on his erection while he masturbated me, making me come all over his chest. He made me lick all this semen off before he'd let me go down on him to suck on his still erect penis while he sucked on mine. We fucked each other later in the night before settling ourselves down to sleep.

We had each other again before breakfast when the male penis is at its hardest and able to give one a real proper fuck, really reaming my insides he did too with it. It was glorious.

'Do you know,' I said as we ate breakfast up in his room, 'you haven't told me where you live or what hospital you work at.'

'Oxford to both questions,' he replied.

'How long can you stay in London?' I asked, hoping it was for a long time.

'Well I can only stay for another three days. I have patients scheduled for later in the week,' he replied. Three days only!

'No longer?' I almost wailed.

'I'm afraid not, so let's make the most of these few days together.' I thought fast and could only come up with one suggestion.

'Why don't you check out of here and spend the rest of the time at my place? You'll like it, and besides, it'll be a damn sight cheaper than here,' I said. He seemed to mull this over. 'It's a good and decent place. No flea pit, I can assure you.'

'Okay,' he smiled and went and phoned down to reception and told them that he would be checking out inside thirty minutes. Oh how nice it would be to finally have a man about the house, I thought, as I helped him get packed, managing to get my ball gown into his suitcase. He carried that and I carried his briefcase as we went down and he paid the bill.

We got a taxi and I gave him my address in Chelsea and off we went and I held his hand the whole short journey. He had a surprised look on his face when we pulled up outside the old Victorian house that I'd had freshly painted a short while back.

'You live here?' he asked as he paid off the taxi.

'It's my home,' I said as I went up the three short steps and opened the door with my key. 'It's a bit sparse on furniture at the moment. I've still got most of what I want in storage but haven't as yet had it delivered.' I led him into the lounge and was pleased that I had bought some good modern stuff and even if I say so myself, it looked a picture.

'It's beautiful. How much rent does it cost if you don't mind me asking?'

'I don't pay rent. It's mine.'

'You own the place? Wow! The agency money must be good then,' and he smiled to take the sting out of what he'd just said.

'The agency money is peanuts. This was bought from an inheritance,' I said. 'Come and see the kitchen.' I took his hand and led him through the dining room, which had a lovely polished table that could seat eight people comfortably, and into my modern kitchen. I'd had the whole place gutted and all new stuff installed and it still looked as good as new.

'Wow again,' he breathed. 'This makes my place look real shabby.'

I laughed. 'You should have seen where I lived before! Now that really was a flea pit. Come, let me take you upstairs and be the first person to see my bedroom.'

We went upstairs and he loved the simplicity and décor of the place and liked the bathroom too. While he was looking in there, I took my dress off.

'Julian,' I said softly as he re-entered the room and saw me standing there in just my female underwear. 'Will you be the first person to make love to me on my bed?'

He didn't need much urging at seeing me like this, for his clothes came off quite fast and I was pleased to see that he already had an erection that he was shortly going to be giving to me. He came into my arms and we kissed as I moved back so that we fell on the bed and then made ourselves comfortable as we kissed and clung to each other, letting our erections make friends again between us.

I was soon up on my knees and had his massive hard tool nuzzle my back passage, knocking at the door and so I relaxed and let him enter. It was glorious to have my backside widened again to accommodate his size and have his shaft keep it wide as he slid right in till our lower bodies met. I loved that pulsating throb and the heat coming from his cock as it fuelled the fire that had been growing inside me since we'd arrived. Now it was up to him to put out the fire and he began moving himself in and out of me, thrilling me as I felt every inch of it move and soothe my inside.

My first lover in my own home and I just loved him for the pleasure he gave me in both of the fucking and the sucking of my cock. For I loved the phallus of a man in either orifice and still couldn't get enough and wondered if I could ever get used to having only one man fuck me. I didn't bring this up until our last day together.

For three whole days, we spent more time on the bed than anywhere else. Fucking each other and then sucking on the opposite prick to wait until it had risen up again. He also liked it when I lay between his legs and took both of his balls into my mouth to roll them around in my attempts to make them generate more of his seed.

In between our bouts of sexual frenzy, he spent some time on the phone calling people he knew in the same profession to find a decent speech therapist who could also help in the singing department. We only left the house twice. Once was to see this man who would try to get me singing again and the other was just to get some food in. Other than that, we stayed half naked most of the time.

It was our last morning together and we'd just fucked each other and were quite content to just lay in each other's arms and kiss and talk.

'Julian. Why don't you move down here to London and get a job in one of the many hospitals here?' I asked of him. 'You could,' I continued when he didn't answer immediately, 'always live here with me.'

'Thanks for the offer Jackie, but I don't think it would work,' he finally said in a low voice. I tried to hide the disappointment these words brought on.

'Why not? I'll cook and clean for you. I'll even darn your socks if I have to,' I said in a pleading voice.

'Jackie,' he said as he stroked my arm. 'As much as I love making love to you and you loving me, it would never work. We'd soon be at each other's throats.'

'Well that's your job,' I said, trying to make a joke of it. 'Why wouldn't it work?'

'If you get your voice back properly and find you can sing again, you'd probably go back into a club.'

'Yes.'

'And what time do you normally get home from there?'

'About two in the morning.'

'Exactly. I get up before five to be at the hospital for my first operation at six. That would be less than three hours in bed together every night.'

'There's the afternoons,' I cried.

'More like early evening before I get away from the hospital and then it would only be an hour or so before you went off to work. That's how I see it and I don't really think that that would be enough for either of us,' he said gently.

I then began to cry for I knew he spoke the truth and realised that I wasn't ready yet to just settle for one man. The twenty-year age gap didn't help either when you look at it. He held me tight as I sobbed and he used the corner of the sheet to wipe my wet cheeks when I'd got myself under control.

'Just come up and see me some time,' I said with a wan smile, trying to sound like Mae West.

'Try and stop me,' he said, giving me our last kiss in bed and I watched as he got dressed, covering that lovely tool that had given me such pleasure. I got out of bed and stayed naked as we went downstairs where I phoned for a mini cab to take him to the station and as we leaned against the front door to wait for it to arrive, we kissed again and he really pleased me by going down onto his knees and sucking on me and urged me on to give him a face fuck, which I did. He came up smiling and I had tears in my eyes again as we passed my sperm back and forth between our lips as we kissed our goodbye and only broke apart at the sounding of a car horn outside.

I couldn't see him properly as he got into the cab for the tears were blurring my vision and with him gone, I went back up to bed and stayed there for the rest of the day, just smelling his body odour that remained on the sheets.

***

Next day, I walked down to the agency and told Samantha that I was back and available but I also told her that I would be taking singing lessons and if I got my voice back again for me to do this, I would be leaving the agency. She didn't like this idea and said so, but wished me luck in the lesson though she didn't want me to go as she was getting more demands for my services.

She got me a booking for that night and I found that he must have been at least sixty years of age and he couldn't understand why I cried when he was fucking me and tried to console me thinking that he'd hurt me but I couldn't really tell him why I cried. Even though he was of that age, he still was able to fuck me once more before going to sleep and then do it again in the morning.

I had my first singing lesson the next afternoon and by golly did my throat hurt after the two-hour session. He kept berating me for trying to sing too high a note and I knew he was right for it turned out into a croak and a coughing fit. We'd started out doing the scales and he kept it right down in almost the range of bass but moving towards the tenor.

'Don't try and hold the notes so long,' he kept telling me. 'You've got to relearn to sing with shorter notes and not go high. Try speaking some of the words instead of singing them and I think you'll find it a lot easier.'

Even so, my throat still hurt but I was going to do this twice a week for as long as it would take. Julian, the sweet man, had tried to pay in advance for my lessons but I wouldn't have that. Telling him that it was my voice and if I failed, I'd rather it was my money that was wasted in the effort.

I was surprised that after three months of the master's tutoring, I was once again singing though in a completely new style from the way I had before. So much for the doctor saying that I wouldn't be able to sing again. When the maestro said that he could do no more for me, I gave him a kiss and took him out for dinner that night to celebrate. I celebrated the following day by going over to Sally's place who simply loved my brown bits and we went and got half pissed and she had to phone the club saying that she was taking the night off. Well, from singing that was, for we went to bed together and made a good night of fucking and sucking each other and as we had gone to bed with full make-up on, we looked a sorry sight the next morning.

She liked the sound of my new voice and said that I would go down a bundle at the club and asked when was I going to see the owner for a slot. I told her that I thought that I deserved a holiday first and this took my mind off on a tangent and thought of that postcard that I'd received from Eddie Forbes.

First it was the passport, and this took three weeks to get and in the meantime, I'd got somebody in an Internet café to do some searching for me of clubs or bars in that area of Murcia that I might get a week's work while I looked for Eddie. We found one and after a lot of toing and froing over the Internet, we agreed on a date and the wage, which was pitiful really, but then, I wasn't really a name that would bring in crowds, besides, it was a bar that could only seat about sixty people. One other thing I was able to screw them down on was that they would put my name quite prominently in the local paper giving the date of my appearance for the week.

This put the date as being in the first week of September when it wasn't too hot and at least the kids would be returning to England for their schooling. I also sent an E-mail to La Azohia hotel booking a room for a couple of days. If I didn't find him then I could always extend the time, for I planned to be over in Spain for a month.

Samantha was unhappy about me giving in my notice whereas the club manager where I used to sing was only too happy to have me back. There was only one thing left to do before my holiday and short stint in this Spanish bar: to buy a pair of trousers and shoes. I couldn't really go through the passport controls wearing a dress when the passport said male.

I was excited when the day finally arrived but by God didn't I just hate putting those trousers on. They were so tight and constrictive and it felt strange wearing that type of shoe once more after getting used to wearing high heels. I took two suitcases with mostly female gear and loads of Euros which I'd got from the bank.

Having checked my atlas and closest airports to my destination, I chose to get the train from Victoria station to Gatwick, because the plane from there would land at San Javier. The Heathrow flights always landed at Alicante, much further north, and as I would be getting a taxi from the airport, it made sense to get as close as I could.

It was a lovely two and half hour flight and my first time in a plane and I thoroughly enjoyed it, especially feeling the power of the engines at the takeoff. We landed about half three in the afternoon their time, for they are one hour ahead of England. I had to show the taxi driver the name of the hotel and where it was on the small map I had and he agreed to take me. It took nearly an hour and cost about fifty pounds but it was worth it for I would never have found the hotel tucked away as it was.

The hotel itself was a garish orange red colour that didn't really go with the environment but inside it was quite modern. Now even though I was wearing trousers, I'd chosen to wear a shirt that could be worn by either sex and in the taxi I had unbuttoned the top few buttons so that the bra I was wearing could be seen so they would assume that I only wore the trousers for travelling.

The reception only gave my passport a brief look to note down the number on my checking-in card. I had the driver bring my two suitcases into the lobby, which was off to the right of this circular domed entrance, it having two upper floors of rooms. I could see the bar off to the left with an open lounge. I paid the driver and as I was given my keys, I asked for someone to carry my bags up to the room for there appeared to be a short-age of staff. I think it was one of the dining room waiters who carried them up for me.

I undressed and had a shower and then got dressed again in clothes that I was more comfortable in, meaning a dress with my high heels. I was gasping for a drink and went straight down to the bar and ordered a large gin and tonic and it was going down a treat when there was a tap on my arm. I turned round and gave out a squeal for it was Eddie Forbes with a lovely deep sun tan.

'Eddie!' I cried and threw my arms round his neck and gave him a kiss.

'Shsss,' he hissed, 'the name's Peter Dawson out here.'

'Well of all things! I came down here to look for you and I'm only here five minutes and you've found me! It's incredible!'

I rapped on the bar for another drink and one for Eddie, no, Peter. I dragged him away from the bar with our fresh drinks to a table where we could talk without being overheard.

'How did you find me so quick?' I asked as we sat down.

'That was easy,' he laughed. 'I saw your name in the local paper that you would be appearing this coming week and guessed that you'd got my postcard. As I'd gently underlined La Azohia, it was only logical that you would book in here. So I tipped the desk clerk some euro's to give me a ring the moment you showed up.' I couldn't help but laugh at how easy I had made it for him.

'There was me thinking that I would have to scour the whole region for you but hoped that I would see you at the bar where I will be singing for the week.'

'So you got your voice back, then? The papers quoted the doctor as saying that your singing career was over.'

'How did you know about that?'

'We do get the English newspapers over here,' he said drily.

'How about you? You've certainly got a nice sun tan. Is it all over?' I asked slyly.

'Would you like to find out?' he asked with a smile.

'Well it goes along with what I came out here for,' I said as I quickly finished my drink and stood up.

He rose from his seat and I led him up to my room and as soon as we were inside, I was kissing him as I fumbled with the belt of his trousers for I could feel that he was hard and ready for me.

'Hello old friend,' I said to his cock as I went down onto my knees and took the head of his prick into my mouth and instantly remembered the taste and smell of him as I sucked and nibbled at the exposed head.

'Steady there,' he said, having to push me away. 'Let's do this properly,' and he quickly took his clothes off and I saw that he was indeed brown all over, but I really only had eyes for that swaying iron bar between his thighs. I only took off my dress and I quickly got a condom out and rolled it down over the length of his shaft and got onto the bed.

He climbed on too and got between my legs and quickly pushed himself up into me.

'Oh God,' I cried. 'You don't know how much I've missed you being where you are now.'

'I've missed you too,' he said as he began to fuck me, moving his prick in and out of me in slow strokes, holding my hips firm as he did so. It was lovely having that hard male penis moving again in my back passage and it made me drool as he gave me the satisfaction that I always got of having a cock up my backside.

'I'm coming,' he grunted though I didn't need telling, as he began to move faster. I began to move back to meet his forward thrusts and he held me tight as he jammed himself tight up to my backside as he pumped out his seed into the condom.

Oh why can't a man hold on longer than a few minutes? It's a pleasure of having a man inside me but it's always too short a duration and

I gave out my cry of dismay when he pulled out. But I was quick to turn round and pull off the rubber and move down and suck and teethed him till he began to wilt. Only when it had really gone soft did I let him out of my mouth and rolled up the bed and into his arms.

'Oh Eddie, I have missed waking up in bed without you there,' I said as I kissed his cheek.

'I've missed you too, Jackie. Now tell me all that happened to you after I left,' he said. So for an hour I related the events, omitting only my other sexual adventures. By the time I was through, he was up and ready for me again. After another glorious fuck, during which I came myself without using my hands, we cleaned each other up and settled down again for him to tell me what he'd been up to since he'd left me.

'The first place I went to was Italy where I knew some people I could trust. There I got me a new passport with a different name,' he began.

'Why? What was wrong with the one I gave to you?' I asked.

'You've heard of the old maxim, set a thief to catch a thief? Well I didn't trust the passport. Too many people would have known about it and so it was wise to get another one. I then flew to Paris and spent a few days there getting to know a few Portuguese truckers and then bummed a lift to Lisbon. From there, it was a case of getting lifts through to here in Spain. Let them try and track my movements from that,' he laughed. 'I released some funds to the lads back in England, enough to keep them going for awhile and got some for myself. So here I am, an expat, living a rather secluded life in the boondocks waiting for someone like you to show up and make me a very happy man.'

'What would make me happy, apart from you having me again, would be something to eat. I'm starving only having had nibbles on the plane,' I said.

'Which do you want first?' he asked, holding up his erection that was again ready for use.

'This of course,' I said as I moved down the bed and took him into my mouth and worked on him with my hand as well, loving the throb and heat of him as I held him there while I sucked and tongued him. He came again and I swallowed it as I would a prairie oyster.

'That was the first course. Now let's get dressed and have something else to fill my stomach.'

We had a shower first before getting dressed and as we got down to the lobby, he steered me out of the hotel.

'I want dinner, not a walk,' I said.

'It's a restaurant that's only a short walk away and it serves better food than the hotel, believe me,' he said.

'But I haven't brought my purse with me,' I said.

'I've got enough in my pocket for dinner,' he said, and we did only walk a little way to a barn-like place that was very Spanish inside and the meal was superb. It was so good that I couldn't eat it all, though I did finish the wine that kept on being put into my glass. He finally called for the bill which was a damn sight cheaper than it would have cost in London and I'm sure not to have been so good to eat. I watched him sort out his euro notes and whispered across to him.

'Eddie. If you're short of money, what with being on the run so to speak, I can let you have a few thousand if it'll help.' He burst out laughing which surprised me.

'Jackie, you really are a treasure. Thank you all the same, but I have enough to manage on. It's you who should be looking after their money. Check out of that hotel in the morning and come and stay at my place. It's the least I can do as you looked after me for a month. How long are you staying in Spain?'

'A month. A week at this bar to get my act together. Three weeks holiday and then back to singing in the club in London,' I said. 'Though if I bomb out here with my singing, I might not return to the club but go back to being an escort.'

'An escort?'

'Yes, and I'm always in demand. You'd be surprised at the number of men who would rather go out with someone such as me for the evening.'

'And for the rest of the night?' he asked with a grin.

'That goes without saying that they give me what I want while they're getting what they want, plus I get paid for it.' Shit! I said to myself. I shouldn't have added that bit on the end, but he didn't comment on that for which I was thankful.

So we walked back to the hotel where he stayed the night with me and he really was a strong man by having me three times during the night and I was slightly sore arsed by the morning. In less than twenty-four hours, he'd fucked me six times and I had him once by way of mouth. Now it takes some man to have that amount of strength to do it that many times inside that timeframe.

The desk clerk didn't like the idea of me booking out after only one night when I'd provisionally booked for two, what with the hotel nowhere near full. Tough tit, I said under my breath and was surprised when Eddie, without asking, picked up their phone and ordered a taxi in fluent Spanish.

'That was bloody quick to learn the language,' I said to him as we waited for the taxi.

'With speaking Italian, it isn't hard to pick up Spanish,' he said, 'for they're all based on Latin and many of the words are similar though with a different pronunciation. Will you be singing any Spanish songs at the pub?'

'I don't know any Spanish songs let alone the words,' I replied.

'How about "Viva Espana?"' he said with a laugh.

'Oh come on! You've got to be joking? That's too corny,' I said, laughing with him.

'Corny or not, I guarantee that will get the crowd in the pub going,' he said, and I found out that he was right when I thought that the place was dying and went and sang it. But that's later.

The taxi arrived and we got in with my suitcases and drove farther into the place called La Azohia for the hotel was just off the main road between Mazarron, well the port, and Cartagena. The road wound round through some nice houses and then ran along the coast until nearly the end for the road finished near a bluff of cliffs and we turned left and went up to a flat section of land that overlooked some houses before the sea with a high mountain behind us. The car turned into a sumptuous villa and I looked at him in amazement that he should be living in such a wonderful place.

It was massive and it had a half-length, Olympic size swimming pool surrounded by a patio that had loungers where you could look out over the pool and see the sea.

'Whose place is this?' I asked as I took in the splendour of the place and the vista it had.

'Mine. Bought and paid for,' he said with a smile.

'Just how much money have you got stashed away?' I asked.

'Oh, about five million, give or take a few quid.'

'And there's me offering you a couple of thousand thinking you might be a bit short of the readies.'

'It was a generous offer Jackie,' he said as he took hold of my hand, 'and I thank you for it. But as you can see, I have enough to live on quite comfortably and get to enjoy the life here in Spain.' I couldn't fault that argument and let him lead me inside which made my place look very small indeed.

'How about a swim?' he asked as he dumped my suitcases down in the big lounge, looking out through the big glass windows at the sparkling clear water of the pool outside.

'I'll get my costume out,' I said, going to my suitcases. 'I had this one specially made with a frill round the crotch and had it padded up top.'

'Costume? How do you think I got brown all over? The nearest house is over two hundred yards away. We're not overlooked at all. It's skinny dipping or nothing. By that I mean you either swim without a costume or it's no swimming at all,' he said as he began to take his clothes off. They were off before I'd even got my dress off. Bare-arsed and really brown all over, he opened the patio window and raced out and dived into the water. It still took me a couple of minutes to get all my hooks undone and with my very pale white body, went and bombed him in the pool.

I came up spluttering and then started to panic because I couldn't feel the bottom having jumped in at the deep end. I couldn't swim and so I panicked and thrashed in the water to try and stay afloat and get to the side. I made it and hung on like grim death, not realising that I had actually done a doggie paddle to get to the edge. He of course had laughed and I didn't think it very funny at the time as I worked my way along the side till my feet touched the bottom.

I rounded on him and ducked him and so for the next hour we played in that marvelously cool water, acting like small children though my idea of a game was different from his. While he kept diving down to try and get my legs and heave me up and over, I kept trying to grab his balls and penis. He tipped me more than I was able to grab him. I liked it also when he came up behind and grabbed me and rubbed himself up against my bum which kept getting me hard and randy.

We eventually got out of the water for he was getting the same way as me and he brought some towels out of a changing room for us to dry ourselves and I laid down on a sturdy wooden lounger that had a thick cushion on it.

'You'll get sunburnt without some oil on,' he said and I saw him take a bottle off the small side table and watched him pour some into his palm and then felt him start to smear it over my back and thighs and eventually caressed my bum with his oily hand.

He must have rubbed some on his erection too, for he then got astride of my lounger and I felt his cock slide up my oiled bum till he was on top of me and felt his prick start to slip between my cheeks. I lifted myself up as best I could with his weight on me and it was enough for his thick cock to push against my entrance and then slide up into me.

The oil made all the difference and I loved the way it moved into me so easily, filling and making me sigh once again at having him there and because of the oil, he lasted far longer than normal as he fucked me there on the lounger. His hands came up under my shoulders to hold me firm as he rode on my back and I loved the slippery feel of his tool moving back and forth inside.

He pulled me firmly down as his thighs mashed mine as he came and I felt every spurt of his seed as he came inside me for he hadn't put on a condom. I gurgled with pleasure at his coming and having him there as he lay fully on my back to get his breath back before pulling out. He went off to the changing room to wash himself before coming back out and laying down on the lounger next to me.

It was simply lovely to lay out there in the sun, having my first real holiday for years, the other times being at my aunt and uncle's home. Though my holiday hadn't really started yet for the next evening I would be singing for my supper.

He only let me stay out there in the sun for two hours before rousing me up from the doze I was having.

'That's enough for you on your first day,' he said, 'otherwise you'll suffer. You've gone quite red already.'

We went inside the villa and into a massive shower that could have held four people. There were jets at all angles coming out of the two walls and I had the pleasure of him soaping me all over and getting the oil off me. Mind you, he spent a long time in and around my bum and other bits. I sensed that he was aroused too and saw I was right when I turned round. I went down onto my knees and took the head of his cock into my mouth and with the water spraying over me, sucked on him and let him face fuck me. It was lovely to taste him again properly when he came in my mouth for me to swallow.

By missing lunch, we had an early dinner and I found that he was a decent cook and the meal was lovely. After which, we went to bed for more and more sex. Though he appeared to be bisexual, he wasn't really one at all for he wouldn't let me fuck him nor would he go down on me. So to help me, he would either jerk me off while still staying inside my rear or lay on top of me and let me fuck the bed whilst again, still inside me, riding me till I came. I didn't mind this for it was him fucking me that was more important or letting me take him in the mouth. Either way, I think I was getting the better deal.

The next day, he let me lay out in the sun for three hours, lying on my back this time to start to brown off the front of me. It's needless to say that he had me twice during the day and an extra one before I did myself up for my first excursion out into the world of singing.

I was quite nervous as we waited for the taxi to pick us up for he was coming with me and knew where we had to go. I poured myself out a large gin and tonic and wanted a second one but decided to wait till we got to the bar. He reminded me that his name was Peter while in Spain and not to slip up and call him Eddie.

The taxi arrived and took us to this club/pub just outside of Mazarron. I can't remember the name of it now, though I know it had an Irish sound. Eddie paid off the driver with the instructions to pick us up sometime after midnight and we went inside. We had a drink at the bar and got to talk to the owner who showed us the stage and dressing room and I passed over my music sheets of the songs that I could sing, letting the pianist pick the order he wanted.

The place was filling up rapidly and it was nearly time for me to start and so I gave Eddie a kiss and went off to the small dressing room to check my make-up and I was then ready and waited with a stomach full of butterflies. I heard the pianist start to run his fingers across the keys and the compere began his spiel about all the way from England etc., and then he announced me as Miss Jackie Trent. I had by now come to the edge of the stage to hear him and remembered that I'd omitted to tell him I was a transvestite. Well you can fool most of the people etc., and with my name being spoken, I stepped out onto the stage to polite applause from the audience and began to sing my first song.

Well it wasn't exactly a standing ovation I got after singing six songs straight off but it was loud enough with some whistles to show that I'd done alright for my first session. My voice was low and throaty and yet still had enough power to be heard quite clearly at the back of the room.

Flushed with pleasure at the applause, I stepped off the stage for a short break and went straight to the bar where Eddie had a drink ready for me.

'Jackie,' he said, giving me a big kiss, 'that was absolutely wonderful! I didn't know you could sing like that!' This pleased me no end. 'I didn't want you to stop and I think the rest of them enjoyed it, it was so…so professional.'

I know I had a big smile on my face and felt thrilled that this first and hardest part had gone so well. I was back singing again and now I didn't want to stop. I finished my drink and went back on stage and sang for nearly three solid hours, giving it all with my heart and even had them singing along to some of the songs.

I was drenched with sweat when I finished my last song of the evening and felt near to exhaustion but still managed to smile and thank them all for being such an enthusiastic audience. The place was still full which proved that my singing hadn't driven them out and round to another bar.

'Well Jackie,' the bar owner beamed at me as he bought me a drink. 'You have a wonderful voice and a unique way of singing and I've not had or heard better ever since I've been running this place. When the word gets round which it most certainly will, we'll have a packed place for the rest of the week. Thanks again,' he finished off, as he moved on to talk to some of the other patrons at the bar.

'Eddie,' I whispered into his ear, 'Take me home and fuck me rigid to knock some of the big headedness that I feel, out of me.'

'I can guarantee the first but not the second, that's for you to learn how to cope with being a success,' he answered me. 'Let's hope the tip was big enough for the taxi driver to be waiting outside for us.' We said our goodnights and left the club/bar to find the cab was indeed there and half an hour later we were at Eddie's villa.

'I could have sung all night, I could have sung all night,' I sang as we entered the lounge, 'and still have begged for more. Now I want to be fucked all night and fucked all night and still will beg for more.' He laughed and poured us both out a drink.

'You can sing all night if you wish but I don't think I can manage the other all night but we'll give it a try,' he said as he took me into his arms and kissed me. 'You were wonderful and I'm sure that many of the men there would like to be in my place now, having you in my arms and getting ready to take you to bed.'

'They'd be in for a shock when finding out that I have parts that a woman doesn't have,' I laughed, kissing him back and pressing my front up to his and finding that he was hard and wanted me. 'Now let's go to bed and give me what I love most and that many men would still want if they ever found out about me.'

He took my empty glass and put it with his on the side and lifted me up and carried me through to the bedroom where he undressed me first before taking his clothes off. I then got what I asked for, a really rough fucking ride, almost brutal and begged him to hold out for as long as he could for I enjoyed this almost rape and cried when he came and pulled out of me. The loss to me was bigger than the cock that had just been removed from my backside. But Eddie was a man amongst men and took me again before we went to sleep.

We fell into a pattern where he would fuck me before breakfast, once again during the morning, after lunch, again in the afternoon and at least twice at night. My sunbathing increased by half an hour a day and the redness began to go and I was slowly turning brown, on both sides.

I was singing every night to a packed bar and positively glowed with the applause I was getting and also began to get offers from some of the men. But taking one look at Eddie, they soon backed off. He had a kind of mien that even though he smiled, other men recognised power when they saw it and so didn't push their luck with chatting me up.

I now had three things I loved. My singing back, a man to fuck me and now I had the sunshine. What else could a girl wish for? I was more a true homosexual than a transvestite for I loved acting as a woman and being fucked by a man, than one who just dresses up as one to sing and act.

Why was I like this, I had asked myself many times but couldn't come up with an answer that made any sense. I was like a nymphomaniac when it came down to it for I just loved the male organ, erect, throbbing and pulsating in either my hand, mouth or stuck up my backside. I just couldn't get enough and that is the crux of the matter. I was still only twenty-one and I knew I had many years yet of having and getting as much of a man's penis inside me before age would start to turn them off. I hoped by that time I would have found the right man, say like Julian, who would have been the perfect match for me if he'd been around my age to start with. Well I had no doubts that that man would finally appear before I got too old, but in the meantime, I was out to get as much as I could.

That week flew by and I was on my last night of singing when the bar owner asked me if I would stay on for another week. I said that I would give him my answer before the end of the night's show and went off to the bar and told Eddie what I'd been asked.

'That's up to you, darling,' he said.

'But I've got another three weeks here in Spain and I'd rather be with you,' I said.

'It's sweet of you to say that Jackie, but your heart is in your singing. Besides, it's only for three hours a night and you'll still have me with you for the rest of the day, and night,' he added.

It was during my last break that the owner came over to us and asked me again if I would do another week for the place was really packed now and I know that many more people would have come if there was room.

'I've discussed your offer with…….' I began and was interrupted by Eddie.

'Miss Trent has agreed to another week providing that her fee is doubled,' he said.

'Done, Miss Jackie,' he said shaking my hand and went off as I turned to Eddie.

'I couldn't have asked for double the money,' I said.

'Well I could. I've been in here before, remember? And I've never seen the place so packed every night of the week. He's making a mint from his bar sales for you being here and bringing them in.'

'Thanks, Eddie. Remind me later to give you an extra one,' I said with a smile.

'An extra one? I can hardly cope with what I'm getting now,' he laughed as he gave me a kiss. 'Now go and do the last session so we can go home for that "extra" one.'

I went off and had the owner announce that I would be staying over for another week, which brought forth a burst of clapping and cheers and I'm not ashamed to admit that I hammed that last bit up by singing "Viva Espana," which went down very well indeed.

So getting my oats still, I went on singing for another week and really enjoyed myself but refused to do another as I wanted two whole weeks of just sex and sunshine, sometimes both at the same time. This I got and I was really a lovely brown all over when those two weeks were up and I fairly clung to Eddie the whole of that last day, well the morning really for I had to leave just after lunch. He wanted to come to airport with me but I said no for it would look strange I said, with me wearing trousers and crying as I kissed him goodbye. Besides, there were always police at the airports and I didn't want him recognised.

He reluctantly agreed to this and I had him fuck me once more after lunch before I got dressed to go. As much as I wanted to start singing in the club in London, I didn't want to leave him and the sun. But we kissed our goodbyes amid my tears and I was driven off in the taxi that he'd hired and already paid for.

I looked at the villa that was next door to his and it wasn't until a year or two later that I learned that Magenta, from the agency, now Lady Bentley, had once stayed there as a friend of the owner, a business tycoon by the name of Sir Malcolm Falconer. *(Ed. Read the story of Lady Magenta, Lady of Pleasure, and Lady of Cuckolds.)*

I was fully composed by the time I got to the airport of San Javier and was glad that I'd made Eddie stay behind for the place was crawling with cops on some alert or other. The security was tight and all luggage was searched but I passed through okay and that place is poxy to spend two hours whilst waiting for your flight and was glad when the call came for boarding.

I had the same thrill at the takeoff and had my face glued to the small window as we did so, to watch the ground flash past ever faster and then to be tilted back into my seat as it soared up into the clear blue sky. The meal served was adequate, having a choice of two dishes served up in a tin foil dish. I paid for some extra drinks to while away the two and a half hour flight.

England felt bloody cold after all that sunshine and nearly seven hours after saying goodbye, I was at Victoria and fifteen minutes later, back in my own home. It seemed so empty without having a man about the place that I just sat down and cried.

Not really knowing what to do with myself, I had a shower and got changed and went out to get pissed. Trust me to pick a night when Chelsea were playing at home at Stamford Bridge, for the pub I finished up in was full of their supporters after having won their game four-one. I got chatted up and being half pissed then, never told the man I walked out of the pub with that I was really a man in drag. He was even more pissed than I was but at least he laughed and saw the funny side of it when I'd taken my dress off to reveal what I was. What the fuck, he'd said. You've got a hole that I can fuck! So we went to bed and I let him fuck me. It's not one that I can really remember and I left his hotel quite early before he woke up and was back home by seven. I had a shower and went to my own bed to sleep away the rest of the morning.

That sleep got rid of any hangover I might have felt for I needed to be at my best for it was this night that I would be singing at the club again. I dressed and took care over my make-up before I took my suitcase with my changes of costumes and went off to the club.

He, the manager, had been prepared for me. Looking at the billboard outside, I found it showed that Sally topped the bill, but plastered across it was a rider announcing my return to sing. I went in and it was like a homecoming, smelling the air of stale smoke and alcohol and went into the dressing room not remembering at how small it was. I was first in and I opened my case and hung my things up and not really knowing my place in there, finally put my cosmetic bag down in the second seat nearest the end opposite the door. Well Sally was the star at the moment and I'm damned sure I wasn't going to be lower than second, for the time being that was, I said to myself.

A few minutes later two new faces came into the dressing room, both about my age and we introduced ourselves as one took the seat nearest the door and the other the third. The room already seemed full with just us three in there but there were still another three to come and the first of those turned out to be Sally.

'Jackie!' she cried as she saw me and pushing past the others came and gave me a hug and a kiss. 'I'm glad you made it. The place has been so empty since you left and look at you! Brown as a berry. All over or have you still got white bits?' She laughed.

'Brown all over, and if you're a good girl, you can see later,' I replied, laughing with her.

'Say no more. Here,' and she moved my cosmetics up to the wall seat. 'That's your rightful place.'

'But you've got top billing,' I protested.

'Not after tonight I won't,' she said with a smile. Now I can truthfully say that Sally is about the only one who would have done or said such a thing for most transvestites can be real bitches when it comes down to it. Sally was one in a million.

I knew the other two girls that came in shortly afterwards and though they weren't bad as singers, they would never ever make the top spot in any club. We said our hellos and got down to the job of changing and putting on our stage make-up. The manager came in during this process to make sure that I had arrived and greeted me warmly and said that he would put me on last, which really was saying that I would be the star attraction.

The music started, which was the cue for the first one to go out and I got her to get one of the waiters to bring me in a large gin and tonic. They slowly went out in turn for their three songs, circulating round the club after their turn on the stage to get the punters to buy them drinks and would not start returning until I went out for my stint.

Sally wanted to hear all about my holiday and how was my voice now?

'Well it knocked spots off them out there,' I said, 'and they even had me do an extra week at double pay. The rest of the time I did a lot of sunbathing. If you come home with me tonight,' I said with a catch in my voice,' I'll tell you the rest and show you my brown bits and you can show me your white ones.' We laughed and then it was her turn on stage and I made sure that I looked good in the mirror for I would be out next. The first girl had come back to repair her face for her turn again when I'd finished with mine.

I went out and stood in the wings as Sally was on her third song and she finished to good applause and came off and gave me a quick kiss on the cheek.

'Knock 'em dead,' she said, as the compere announced that after a long period without the singing sensation of London etc., well he did go rather over the top sometimes, and then almost screamed out my name and I went out into the spotlight to a really good round of applause and whistles.

After the first song finished, I knew I had them eating out of my hand. I'd sung so well, with my new voice of course. They even stood and clapped me at the end of my third and as I left the stage to circle about, I was being offered drinks left, right and centre and the best of all was that they all wanted to take me out to the cottages.

I saw many old faces and I couldn't keep the smile off my face and finally sat down with one of my old regulars and accepted a drink from him. Sid, his name was and he'd always been in once a week when I was last at the club and I think he only came so that he could have the pleasure of fucking me.

'We've really missed you, Jackie,' he said, putting his hand over mine. 'Do you still, er, you know? I've been saving my money up knowing that you would come back one day.'

'Thank you Sid and yes, but this will be a freebie for old times' sake,' I said as I stood up. His smile was lovely at hearing this for he must have been at least sixty and I think that coming to the club and paying their high prices was purely to come and have the fuck of the week with me. He followed me out to the toilets, getting envious looks from other men for being the first to have me on my return. Inside, Sally had just dropped her dress down and her punter was still trying to pull his zipper up, slightly red in the face and knowing that we knew what he'd just been doing.

'Nice one Sid,' Sally said with a smile as she followed her man out, leaving us alone. I bent over the basin and lifted up the hem of my dress and I heard Sid's zipper come down and then he fumbled with his condom and then I felt the head of his cock nuzzle my backside, the first time for nearly a year, and gushed at how big he'd grown when he started to push himself into me. I gathered he liked this comment for he held my hips firm as he began to move and fuck me.

He was good and I think because of his age, he could last longer than most men and it was nice to once again have a cock reaming my backside. But he still came too soon for my liking and he pumped hard at my rear as he shot his load and leaned on me somewhat as he fought to get his breath back. I gave out my usual cry when he pulled himself out of me and I quickly turned round and told him that I would give him a bonus for loyalty and pulled off his condom and went down onto my knees to suck on his cock and draw out the residue that was still inside. He was over the moon with having had me two ways and not having to pay anything.

In fact, I had twelve men fuck me that first night and I sucked on all of them and didn't charge them a penny, such was my joy at having so many admirers who were glad to see me back. I even had one remark on my brown cheeks and he kissed both of them before sticking his prick in between them to fuck me.

To say I was a hit that night is somewhat of an understatement if you don't mind me saying. I was back on top form and was really clapped and cheered every time I appeared out on the stage. We all bowed after the finale and some of the girls took their wigs off to show that they were males though I couldn't for my hair was my own and looked better than some of the wigs worn.

'There's no two ways about it Jackie,' Sally said when we were back in the dressing room to clean off the stage make-up which is much thicker than what one normally wore for being outside. 'You definitely deserve the top spot. Your voice is even better than it was before. So throaty and gravely and ever so sexy. It nearly made me come just looking and listening to you and I'm an old pro now at this game.' Now this was really an accolade for I knew that she meant ever word of it.

'You are coming home with me tonight?' I asked.

'Oh yes. I want to see this brown bum of yours,' she said with a smile. So with us dressed and ready, we left the club and took a taxi to my place and this would be the first time for Sally to see where I now lived.

'Hey! We're going the wrong way,' she said to me as she noticed we were not heading south.

'No we're not. I forgot to tell you that I've moved to a new place. I bought it with the money that my aunt left me,' I said.

'Well to be frank, it'll probably be better than the place you did live in,' she said.

'You're not wrong there,' I replied smugly.

'Well Chelsea has a better post code than the last place,' she said as we pulled up outside. 'And you've got your own front door instead of a shared one,' she added as we got out of the taxi and I paid him off.

'Wait until you see inside. It's even better,' I said as I unlocked the door and led her in. She positively gushed with every room that she walked into, me following along behind her grinning like a Cheshire cat. I saved my bedroom till last and she loved it, especially as it had its own en suite bathroom.

'Last year you lived in a flea pit, was knifed and lost your voice and now you're singing again, have a new house and pots of money. I'm just so fucking jealous but I still love you,' she said as she gave me a kiss to prove it.

'While we're in here, do you want to see my brown bits?' I asked, going a little coy. 'Then we can go to bed and you can find the little brown place that's always been there.'

'Oh yes,' she breathed and quickly took her dress off and watched me take off mine. 'Wow,' she said. 'Turn round.' I did a little turn for her. 'Brown, even where the sun doesn't shine. Oh God, where are the condoms? You look so gorgeous standing there I can't wait.'

We were still in our underwear and I turned and could see that she was up and ready to fuck me and so we both sat down and peeled off our stockings, belt and bra. Neither of us wore any panties and I got a condom out for her as I got onto the bed in my favourite position. Sally got onto the bed behind me and stroked the brown cheeks of my bum.

'How many men did you have tonight?' I asked as I felt the tip of her erection press between those cheeks of mine.

'Six, and you?' she asked as the head of her cock widened me and slipped inside, making me gurgle with delight.

'Twelve. You're making it thirteen,' I said as her thighs came up to mine and she was fully inside me.

'That's an unlucky number,' she said as she began to move herself in and out of me.

'Then you'll have to fuck me twice to make it fourteen then,' I said with pleasure. She wasn't as adept as me in holding back but was still able to last three times as long as any other man, moving her cock back and forth as she rogered me. I was loving it and had to fight the urge to come myself, saving it for her. She held my hips tight as she started to come and rammed into me with short sharp stabbing motions until she stiffened and let just her hips keep pumping her seed out into the rubber.

After the hated withdrawal, I was quick to pull the condom off and suck on her still steaming cock to taste her again. Then it was my turn and I just loved pushing my own cock up into her arse hole and feel the tight-ness of her insides. Far tighter than any woman and therefore you got more feeling out of it as you fucked somebody's backside. I lasted nearly ten minutes of moving my shaft inside her, running my hands up and down her back making her shiver before I held her tight and rammed hard into her as I finally came. Like me, she peeled off the rubber and went down on me, sucking and licking me till I was clean.

We then got under the covers of the bed and held each other as we kissed and cuddled. I told her all about Spain, or what I saw of it and being fucked every day quite a few times but not mentioning Eddie's name but only called him Peter. Also of how my singing went down at the bar that thought it was a club.

'And nobody twigged that you were a male artiste?' Sally asked.

'No. It was only Peter that knew, well he would, wouldn't he. He thought it was funny the way some of the men there tried to chat me up but he was my excuse for not sampling others. I wonder how many would have carried on if they only but knew what was under my dress, but then, most of them were middle aged and older, no really young ones. We should do a tour one day and have some fun while getting you brown all over like me,' I said, which she thought would be a good idea.

By now, as we'd been playing with each other's cock, we were ready for another session and it was even better having already gotten our rocks off once and lasted a bit longer, the pair of us. After the sucking and licking and a goodnight kiss we settled down to sleep and I asked her if she would like to move in with me.

'There's another bedroom if you want to sleep on your own some nights.'

'I'd love to,' she replied enthusiastically. 'How much rent would you charge me?'

'No rent, but if you bought the food and drink for us two, I'll see to paying all the other bills,' I said, knowing that the cost of that food and drink would still be less than what she was paying now for her place, plus she had the other bills to fork out. This didn't leave her much from her wages from the club so it was a good offer. Well we'd known each other for nearly ten years and we were good in bed together and got on well at work so I thought it was a good idea.

It was nice to wake up in the morning and feel another body lying alongside and to put your hand over the thigh and find a rampant prick. Sally stirred as I began to move my hand up and down on her shaft, feeling that morning strength in it and she turned slightly towards me, not being fully awake and I went down under the covers and took the head of her cock into my mouth and sucked on it as I worked it with my hand.

'That's lovely,' I heard her say as the legs stretched beneath me. I kept on sucking and squeezing that hard cock until I felt her tremble and the sperm shot out into my mouth. I kept my lips firmly clamped round the head so's not to lose a drop and when she'd finished coming, I swallowed most of it but kept some in my mouth to pass across to her as I kissed her after coming up from down under.

'So you've had your breakfast, now I'll get mine,' she said and disappeared beneath the covers and I loved how her hot mouth closed over the head of my cock and began to suck and tease it as she used her hand. I lifted my hips up as I came, filling her as she did me and knew that I would be getting a taste, which I did when she surfaced and kissed me.

'I'm going to love living here with you Jackie,' she said, giving me a cuddle, and so she was effectively living with me from that point on.

We fucked each other during the afternoon and went off to work together and I got another rapturous applause when I went out onto the stage to start my first session that evening.

No freebies tonight and I still had men waiting to take me out to the cottages to fuck me or have me suck their dicks. There's nothing like pulling down the zipper of a man's trousers and pulling out a hard erection and feel him shiver with my hand being cool. Then he would tremble as I knelt down and blew into the winking eye of his cock before giving it first a kiss before taking it into my mouth and begin to suck on it. Sometimes I was able to get his balls out too and I would fondle these as I worked my head on his cock and hold him hard and rub quite fast when he began to shudder as he came. They nearly all tasted the same and it was nice to get a full load that was worthwhile swallowing.

The other part was to pull out the hard erection and roll a condom down over the head and shaft and then turn round and flip up the back of my dress and feel his hand hold my hip whilst his other guided the tip of his tool to my entrance. When it was there he would then bring this hand up to my other hip as he pushed himself forward and I just loved the feel of the head of his cock widen my hole and then slip inside and have the rest of his throbbing cock enter me and he would hold himself tight up to my backside for a momentary pause before he began to move himself and fuck me.

It was lovely to get what I loved and get paid for it too. How much I had missed being away for I averaged about ten a night and so made quite a tidy sum over the week, far more than I was being paid to sing.

My singing had never been better and the club was full every night so the boss was making a lot of money too. We also had Sally's twenty-first birthday in the club after our night's work, letting a few regulars stay and we all got quite pissed and if we were not being fucked by the regulars who stayed, we finished up fucking each other and didn't leave the club till six in the morning.

It was a few weeks later that I got a surprise at the club. I had done my first stint of the night and took two men out back to be fucked by them and when I came off the stage after my second time up there, I saw Julian sitting at one of the tables.

'Julian!' I cried out and quickly went and sat down at his table. I didn't kiss him then though I would really have liked to. 'Why didn't you phone and tell me you were coming? I would have taken the night off to be with you,' I said as I took hold of his hand under the table and gave it a squeeze.

'I wanted to see and hear you sing without you knowing that I was here,' he said, giving my hand a squeeze back. 'You've got a wonderful voice, so vibrant and mellow. It gave me the shivers just to hear you. So the singing lessons paid off, I'm glad and very pleased for you.'

'Julian, I thank you with all my heart for what you did for me and you've heard the result. Without your encouragement, I wouldn't be here tonight. How long are you in London for and can you stay the night?' I asked, hoping that the answer was yes.

'I'm only here for the night for I have to be back at the hospital tomorrow and yes, I'd love to stay the night with you,' he said and my bum gave itself a squeeze and a twitch at his saying yes.

'How lovely, though I'm sad it's only for one night. Don't drink any more of that crap,' I said as he went to pour me out a glass from the bottle he'd bought. 'Let's have a decent drink.' I beckoned over a waiter and told him to get rid of the bottle and bring us some proper drinks and that I would be paying. This meant that I would only have to pay the correct price and not what the punters would normally pay. Having Julian there stopped me from cruising the tables for the rest of the evening, but what the hell.

I did the rest of my songs and he clapped as loudly as any of the others that were there. I sat with him in between my sessions and he was waiting for me when we'd finished for the night and as I was doing my make-up, realised that I hadn't told him about Sally living with me. I told her that he was there and she said that she didn't mind for she could always sleep in the other bed for the one night.

I introduced them when we went out into the club to collect Julian, and he was a bit disconcerted when I said that Sally was living in the house with me. Nothing was said in the taxi home and when we were in the lounge, I poured us out some drinks and laid it on the line for Julian.

'I'm sorry to have sprung this on you at the last minute Julian, but Sally is the same as me, and, well, we do normally sleep and have sex together. She's the only one who knows about us so please don't worry, the secret is ours.'

It seemed strange to now have a person in the house wearing trousers when both of us were wearing dresses and I then had a lovely thought. 'As much as I love you Julian, I also love Sally,' I said as I went and sat down beside him and took his hand. 'I'm turfing her out of my bed for you and she has agreed because of what you have done for me. But wouldn't it be nice to try being a threesome? It's something I've never done before and I think it could be quite exciting.' I held my breath and hoped he would say yes to this proposal.

'Well I feel somewhat embarrassed now as it is,' he stammered.

'Oh Julian, come now. If you face the facts, we are all sisters under the skin so there shouldn't be any embarrassment at all. Why not make this night one to remember, and maybe it would make you come to London more often?'

'My position......'

'Your position,' I interrupted, 'is to be behind and fucking me. I'd like to have another cock in front of me to suck on at the same time. It's something I've often dreamt about and you could make it come true. We could even make a daisy chain! Think of it. You stuck up inside Sally here and me stuck up inside of you! Now that would be some fuck to remember,' I finished off.

'Julian,' Sally spoke up. 'There's only one way I can thank you for what you've done for Jackie and that is to offer myself.'

'Thank you, Sally, you've just given me an offer that would be churlish to refuse,' he smiled.

'I'm just like a Godmother,' she said and stood up with her hands on her hips and tried to imitate an American gangster. 'I made him an offer he couldn't refuse. Do I look like a moll?'

'Flanders?' Julian queried with a smile.

'Did you see it on the telly? Oh I wish I had tits like she had,' Sally said wistfully, 'instead of this padded bra, which I'm now going to take off.'

'No!' said Julian hoarsely and rather hastily, 'Stay….stay in your underwear. You too, Jackie.'

'For you my sweet,' I said rising up and giving him a kiss, 'I'll bend over backwards, though I think forwards would be better,' I finished with a laugh and took hold of his hand and heaved him out of the chair he was sitting. 'And so to bed, as Samuel Pepys quoted,' I said.

'You sure it wasn't that fella in Kiss Me Kate?' asked Sally as she got up too and followed us into the bedroom. To set Julian at his ease, I took my dress off straight away and was unable to hide the erection I had as I helped Sally off with hers. She too had her cock upright and bouncing about in anticipation. I started to undress Julian and Sally joined in and we soon had his clothes off and he too was rampant and Sally and I both went down onto our knees to pay homage to man's gift to women, or males like us. We both kissed and licked at his organ until he cried out that that was enough or he would waste what he had.

We both quickly rose up and scrambled onto the bed and waited for him to climb on the bed and find out who he wanted to mount first. To save any embarrassment over his choice I told him to fuck Sally first and would he like it if I fucked him at the same time, being the driving force as it were.

This suggestion was agreeable and so Sally rolled a condom onto Julian's prick while I put my own on and Sally turned round and presented her backside to Julian who shuffled forward on his knees behind her. Sally gave out a gurgle as he pushed himself inside her.

'Now lean over her,' I said to him, which he did and I then was able to see my target and I quickly pushed myself up into Julian.

'Oh my God! This is fantastic,' he cried as I buried my cock deep inside him. I held his hips as he held those of Sally as I began to move.

'Here we fucking go!' I cried out as I started to fuck Julian, my movements making him do the same to Sally.

There were grunts, groans and gasps as we moved in unison in our coupling. He was tighter than I remembered and I loved every minute of sliding my cock in and out of his arse and slowly built up the momentum till I cried out that I was coming. Julian cried out as I rammed myself hard into him as I came and he in turn shot his load and Sally gave out a gurgled scream as the weight of two of us bore her down onto the bed.

We lay there gasping one on top of another until Sally called out from underneath.

'What about me coming? Ease up but stay inside him Jackie,' she said. I slowly levered myself up as Julian rose up too, pulling out of Sally who gave out a cry at the angle of withdrawal. 'Now stay like that for a moment,' she said as she slipped out from under us and quickly got herself a condom and got back onto the bed behind me. 'Now it's our turn,' she said as she moved forward.

I felt her cock push up to me and I relaxed as best I could and felt her cock slide up into me. So I was now the meat in the sandwich and as Sally fucked me with my own cock once again reaming Julian's backside. She came with some force but alas, I didn't have any left, but it was still good in having my cock moving about inside Julian. She cried out as she came and once again, we fell into a heap on the bed with Julian now on the bottom.

We slowly, after several minutes, began to separate to much sucking sounds as pricks were pulled out of backsides and the condoms were pulled off. It's very difficult the first time, to lay and be in the right position as we formed a triangle of our bodies so that we could suck on a still erect penis. It was awkward but we managed to take one in our mouth to suck one whilst our own was also being sucked. A threesome is great!

It was also nice later, to be on your knees and have a throbbing prick up your arse fucking you whilst you had another rampant cock to suck on at the same time. I was overjoyed at having both ends filled at the same time with Julian fucking me while I sucked on Sally.

It was close to dawn before we'd finally been able to let all have this experience and we fell asleep exhausted and with the knowledge that we'd all been well and truly fucked out of our minds. It was late morning when we woke up in a tangle of limbs and none of us had the strength for any more at the time. So after giving Julian a hasty late breakfast, he left us in a taxi, promising to visit us again as soon as he could. He'd given both of us a kiss and I hoped that he didn't have any major surgery planned for that afternoon for he would surely have fallen asleep while doing it. As for us, we went back to bed to sleep till the late afternoon.

That's how my life is progressing at the moment. I have an untold number of cocks shoved up my arse in the evenings at the club and Sally sees to me twice a day. We occasionally have one of the other girls round for a night of being a threesome but that is really tiring so we don't do it very often. Julian visits us about every three months and that is enough…

Enough? What I can never get enough of is being fucked by a rampant and throbbing prick and I just hope that I will get enough before I become too old to enjoy it as I do now. Why am I finishing the story at this point? That's a good question and I can't really come up with an answer, so let's just leave it as Why?

THE END

Here is a sample from another story you may enjoy:

AMY REDEK

His SPECIAL LESSONS

Quentin College was a place that I had taken a fancy to when I was studying for my doctorate at University and was very pleased when I received a letter asking me to attend an interview. I was one of twenty there that day and I progressed into the next interview of ten and finally for a third visit of just three of us for a position in such a prestigious college.

I was the last to be interviewed and I went into the Dean's office to find two other people sitting there along with the Dean himself, who had been present at my two previous visits. He was sitting behind his large desk and flanked by a man on his right and a woman on his left. I knew of them through my studies and the newspapers but waited until I was formally introduced to them before speaking.

'Sit down, Dr. Smith,' Dean Ainsworth said, indicating the chair placed before the desk. 'I am pleased to see that you made it to the last three and through your work, I'm sure you know Mrs. Cynthia Carrington who is attached to the Department of Education in the present government.' I nodded in her direction and gave her a small smile. 'And Sir Reginald Hudson, who, though in opposition at the moment, is the Chairman of the College Board of Governors.' I nodded in his direction and gave him the same smile.

'To recap for their benefit, you were born on the 14th May 1974 in London, christened Colin Franklin Smith and are now twenty-six years of age with both parents now deceased. You won high honours at college and obtained your doctorate at Oxford in the field of Political History on a brilliant thesis showing the parallels between the English Civil War and the American war of Independence. You have also written a book using these lines, which I myself have read and have ordered copies for the college library.

Now having seen you twice previously, I'll let my esteemed colleagues put forward their questions as to why you think you are fit for the position in this college. Mrs. Carrington, if you would be so kind as to lead off.'

He sat back with a smile on his face and listened to the questions that were fired at me for over half an hour and to my answers. They were very demanding and I gave the best answers that I could and felt mentally drained when it was over and shook hands all round before I left, being told that I would be notified within a week if I'd succeeded to the post or not.

I went back to London to my home in Chelsea. A house in Cheyne Walk left to me by my parents two years ago. My father had been a cardiac consultant, but his profession did nothing for him for he died of a heart attack at the age of sixty-one. Mother, with his loss, just seemed to pine away and so followed him two years later, but it was recorded as natural causes in her case.

That was two and a half years ago and so I went off to America to further my education in my field and had only been back in England for three months before applying for this doctorate post of Political History at Quentin College. In the States, I had attended Yale University, and by having the other side of the story as it were about what led up to the War of Independence, prompted me to write my thesis.

True to their word, I received a letter a week after my last interview from Dean Ainsworth congratulating me on securing the post and could take up residence whenever I wished for the incumbent had already retired. It was two weeks into the summer holidays and another four weeks before the new term year began; and as I didn't have any ties, immediately packed all that I would need and set off for the college.

Before the taxi driver could even begin to grumble about helping me get my two trunks down to his cab, I gave him a fiver and then had him drive me to the station where I had to get a porter to get them to my platform. The train I wanted was there and people were already boarding and I just had enough time to get my ticket and see the trunks put into the guards van.

If you enjoyed this sample then look for **His Special Lessons**.

Also by this Author:

The Painted Sword

Cruise Control

Wild Pleasures

Lending My Beloved

Lady of Cuckolds

Lady of Pleasure

Lady Magenta

Sexually Overdosed

Meeting My Fancy Dear

Prison Sex Slave

Chasing A Shadow

The Hostel

The Island

Thirst for Drugs and Pleasure

Forgotten Identity

Grey Memories

Chronos: Time Machine

The Hard Bomber

Honeymoon Abduction

The Yacht Sins

Summer at the Villa

Practice Makes Perfect

Stranger Danger

Following Father's Footsteps

The Square Circle

The Wizard of Kos

Coming Together

Out in the Real World

Me, Carol and Raoul

Under the Mistletoe

Play House

A Cocktale for Sherry

Loving Rhett

Farell

Homos Ubique

Foxhole

Deaf, Dumb and Blind

Loving the Mechanic

Up for Sale

No White Snow

Love Motel

A Man's Toy

From the Author

WANT FREE COPIES OF MY BOOKS?
Just visit my blog and download free copies of my books:
amy-redek.awesomeauthors.org/amy-redek

Author Central – http://www.amazon.com/Amy-Redek/e/B00A48NQ72

If you enjoyed any of my books then please share the love and click like on my books in Amazon. Your reviews are greatly appreciated.

One Last Thing, For Kindle Readers...

When you turn the page, Kindle will give you the opportunity to rate this book and share your thoughts on Facebook and Twitter. If you enjoyed my writings, would you please take a few seconds to let your friends know about it? Because... when they enjoy they will be grateful to you and so will I.

Thank You!

Amy Redek
amy_redek@awesomeauthors.org

About the Author

George Eliot was a famous writer, though at the time, only male authors were recognised. It was in fact the pen name of Mary Ann Evans, a female.

When I started writing, I thought that if a woman could use a male name, why, with me being male, why couldn't I use the name of a female? Though to be different, I made my writer's name from an anagram of my real name.

I wasn't the brightest spark in my school days and it was only while being in the Merchant Navy did I self-educate myself. That being mostly literature, classical music and artists, like Tolstoy, Chopin and Rembrandt. After leaving the navy, I had several jobs, finishing up by being a working boss using my own maxim that 'Management is the art of delegation.'

It's when I became self-employed that I began to write, though sadly, not many of my books can be published because of certain laws that forbid certain aspects of life. This never fazed me for I was really writing just to please myself having a wide range of the human psych.

Having written ninety stories, my only aim now is to reach one hundred. I give thanks to the publishers for at least putting some of my efforts out for others to enjoy as much as I did in the writing of them.

You may also like the books by these authors:

DICK PARKER

SPRING BREAK
VIDEO

HOT GAY EROTICA

GAY PORN COLLEGE SUPER STARS 2

I was home early from classes so I packed the orders that needed to be sent out for Boner Boys, a video my friends and I had made last summer. As I printed out the mailing labels I noticed that we'd hit a milestone. We had a program that added each mailing label to a growing list of previous customers and these nine had taken us over the twelve thousand five hundred mark to 12,506.

"Holy shit! We've made a quarter of a million dollars on it," I thought to myself.

What had started out as a lark, just fooling around with my friends Mark and Tony had turned into moneymaking industry. The two of them and my boyfriend Jarred and I had taken a gay video to the market thinking we'd maybe make enough sales to buy some beer for our shared apartment at college and it had turned into an amazing success that had turned us into very well-off students.

I sat back in my chair and thought back to that spring day when Mark and Tony and I had finished our video for a high school project. We'd joked around about making a porno and one thing led to another and before we knew it Tony was lying naked on a blanket in the woods with Mark jacking him off.

Mark was a mid-weight wrestler in high school who had many girls and girlfriends during his high school years. He was a stud, with blond hair, blue eyes and a killer six-foot body with muscles in all the right places.

Tony was a bit shorter and with dark curly hair who was really well built and handsome as hell. Tony was a cock hound and not too fussy about whether he got off with a guy or girl.

I, on the other hand, was decently built and decent looking but not a jock type. I was probably the least outgoing of the three of us and I had a secret. I was gay.

We joked around about making a porno and I suggested there were no girls we could talk into it so we should make a gay one. At first they were a bit shocked but eventually they both got into it and we filmed the first scene with Mark jacking Tony off.

I was surprised at how they both got into it. The second scene was of me. I was standing in the woods with my pants down and my shirt off jacking off. Tony just happened to be sauntering through the woods and spied me. So he snuck up behind me and took over jacking me off.

That scene ended up with cum all over the place. The video grew from there to sucking cock and eventually to fucking. Along the way we added my boyfriend Jarred. He and I had been fucking around for about a year but no one knew. Jarred was another wrestler who was one of those little guys who was only about five-foot-three and a hundred pounds. He was a cute little shit with blond hair and a hell of a cock for such a little guy. He was a complete hound for cock.

We ended up with a pretty damn good video, put some clips on some of the free porn sites and started getting orders.

We sold the video called Boner Boys, for $20. We charged $6 for shipping and handling and that paid for the cost of copying the video, and the shipping with a little left over, so we made $20 a pop.

We had no idea that so many orders would come in. After a week we had to buy an extra computer to burn discs, and a bigger printer to print the labels and covers.

When we started college in the fall we rented an apartment together and set up a workroom where we could make copies and produce the videos every day after classes.

By the time we started school Mark and Tony were boyfriends. Mark had always had a curiosity about gay stuff and found he liked it better than girls. Tony was still bisexual but was pretty exclusive with Mark. Jarred and I were in love.

The four of us had a hell of a good time in our apartment and were amazed every day by the amount of orders we got for the video.

Eventually we formed a company called Fun Video, and set up a corporation. At first we bought blank DVD discs from Walmart but it didn't take long to realize we needed bigger quantities so we set up accounts with a company and bought our supplies by the thousands.

Today was a milestone. With 12,500 orders we had hit a quarter of a million in sales. Just about all of it was profit. Life was good.

I stacked the outgoing orders by the door on a table and took a shower. When I finished I slipped on some clean boxers and turned on TV. I lay back against the couch with my bare feet up on the coffee table and started watching Pawn Stars.

It didn't take long and I fell asleep and began to dream. I was lying on a soft bed in my dream and my cock was hard. I could feel my hand on it and knew I was jacking off. Then I felt a hot mouth on it and I moaned. The dream was very realistic.

The hot mouth felt great and my dick was hard as hell and it didn't take long and I got the feeling that I was about to cum. I started shooting cum and woke instantly. Holy shit, what a dream!

Then I looked down and that fucking Jarred was kneeling naked on the floor in front of the couch with my dick in his mouth.

"What the hell?"

"Hi, sweetie," he said looking up and smirking.

"What the fuck are you doing?"

"I'm pleasuring you."

I had to grin. Jarred looked like he was about sixteen but he was really nineteen, like the other three of us. He wore his blond hair in a Justin Bieber hairstyle that made him look even younger.

Although he was compact, his years as a lightweight wrestler had given him a killer body and a cute little ass that I just adored. His cock was pretty damn big for such a little shit, being a good six inches hard. He and I had started messing around in high school and when he joined our little video company we really had a lot of fun. He was funny and spontaneous and not afraid to do anything.

My cock was really sensitive from Jarred sucking me off.

"Let go of it," I said pulling away.

"Tickly?'

"Damn tickly."

He stood up with his nice boner right in my face. The tip was shiny with pre-cum.

"Have a taste?" he asked grinning.

I leaned forward and opened my mouth and took him right to the pubes. I'd sucked Jarred's cock many times and it was perfect for sucking and for getting fucked with. Oh, I know big huge cocks are impressive but a nice six-inch one that is medium a thickness is a lot more practical when it comes to sex.

Jarred closed his eyes and moved forward. I played with his balls and squeezed his beautiful butt cheeks. He had a killer ass.

"Oh, Richie, that feels so good," he whispered.

I went really deep and clenched at his cock with my throat. He shuddered.

"Will you look at that?"

I looked out of the corner of my eye and there stood Mark and Tony in the doorway.

"I believe that boy on the couch is trying to blow up that other boy. Maybe he has a leak," Tony said using some kind of a hillbilly voice.

"Could be. Maybe he's filling the boy on the couch with some kind of fluid or something. Maybe his radiator is low."

"Shut the fuck up! You're ruining the mood," Jarred said grinning.

"I'm feeling a little low. Maybe you'd like to blow me up too," Tony said looking at Mark as he shut the door.

"I'd surely like to try."

The moved over by us, and both got naked. Mark's big seven-inch cock was standing up and he sat on the couch while Tony stepped in front of him with his curved six-and-a-half-inch boner. He had a big drop of pre-cum on the end. Mark leaned forward and took half of it into his mouth.

Mark and I sucked our buddies and they stood there grinning at each other. Tony reached over and fondled Jarred's ass cheeks and Jarred played with Tony's right nipple.

"How about this?" Tony asked. He slid his hand down Jarred's butt and slipped his middle finger in his ass crack.

"Oh fuck!" Jarred gasped. His cock began to throb and he filled my mouth with cum.

I milked him dry and he pulled away from me. He leaned down and kissed me.

"Gotta get Tony off," he said.

"Of course it's the neighborly thing to do," I said grinning.

He knelt behind Tony and spread his butt cheeks. He leaned in and I knew he had his tongue in Tony's hole.

"Oh man," Tony said loudly. Then Mark jumped and I could see him swallowing.

I leaned down and took Mark's big cock in my mouth and started sucking him. He finished Tony off and then Tony joined me and sucked Mark's nuts as I sucked his dick. Jarred got up on the couch and put his limp dick up so Mark could suck on it.

It didn't take long and Mark came in my mouth. We all were a little out of breath and Jarred had a boner again.

The three of us started sorting through the mix of clothes on the floor and Jarred stood there holding his boner.

"What am I supposed to do with this?" he said waving it around.

"Shove it up your ass," Tony said.

"Oh yeah, easy for you to say."

"Come on, someone suck me off."

We all sat there grinning. What a horny little shit…

If you enjoyed this sample then look for **Spring Break Video**.

CHRIS JOHNS

Take it

OFF

HOT GAY ROMANCE EROTICA

The advert was quite specific.

Male pole dancers and strippers required for late night private members club. Don't apply if you have any inhibitions concerning nudity and displaying your wares.

Paul Hancock had just been made redundant and sat outside his apartment was a brand new BMW. Paul would do just about anything to keep it but without a job he wouldn't be able to meet payments. Despite having a good job for years, the only thing Paul owned was his flat. Everything else was the subject of hire purchase contracts, especially the Beamer.

The prospects of getting another well-paying job quickly were slim to non-existent. The best he could hope for was here in front of him. If he did this job he would be free during the day to job search. Although he wouldn't have said so himself, Paul was every gay man's wet dream and instant wet pussies on girls. His only problem was that he was shy and for this, the last thing he would have to be was shy, but where needs must.

With his heart in his mouth, Paul attended at the designated time and was surprised how many guys were there for auditions. They were led in to the main club and told to make themselves comfortable.

"The joint owners will see you one at a time but first will you fill in the form that is on all the tables. Also, take a Polaroid picture of yourself to attach to the form."

They made a game of taking the photos somehow eased the tension in the room.

"Now I don't want all you ladies getting excited when I pose for this picture", said one of the boys, as he slipped his shirt off one shoulder and got into a very provocative pose. They all laughed and fooled around in the photos.

When it was job done, the auditions started. The first one came out looking scared to death and told the others what was going to happen.

"I'm not staying. After you strip naked the girls start playing with you to get you hard, and they play with your arse as well."

He left, joined by several others. The five that were left looked at each other until one guy spoke.

"Huh, they won't get any joy from me. Women turn me right off."

Paul gulped and asked, "Are you gay then?"

The guy laughed and said, "Yeah, queer as a nine bob note," (no such thing of course).

He was the next one summoned and came out looking very pissed off.

"Bitches, they don't want me because I wouldn't get hard for them."

Four to go. One of the owners came through then looking less than happy.

"Something for you to think about. We'll do the rest of the auditions here. While we do them think about this. The club is a high end club for rich bitches like me, who want slutty action. You will be played with and you'll do two shows per night. The pay is £500 per night plus whatever tips you get, and they can be substantial."

One guy summed it up for the remainder.

"They can fuck me for that."

The owner smiled and came back.

"I'm pleased to hear that because they do like to see man on man sex culminating in someone getting a cock up their arse. The stripper that takes it usually gets tips that are more than his pay so give it some thought."

"Now, Paul, up on the stage, strip to the music that will start for you, use the pole and make it as raunchy as you can. If you get the job we'll supply special clothes and coaching to make it more erotic, but for now, do your best."

Paul was quite a good mover on a dance floor and started off with the music, no problem. He slowly undid his shirt and peeled it off throwing it at the audience of guys and the boss girls.

Using the pole he was able to toe off his shoes without having to bend, keeping the moves going. Trousers were next. He unclipped the top and slowly pulled down the zip. As they slid down his legs he grabbed the pole and swung round on it, kicking his trousers off as he did so. This next bit would test his resolve as he blushed almost scarlet. Now clad in just a pair of mini briefs and his socks one of the other guys, who was also gay, whistled and cat called and the boss girls clapped. Paul stopped then looking very embarrassed.

"You need to keep going if you want this job, pants off and a solid erection while you keep dancing and then you jump off the stage and start circulating being as erotic as you can for the clients."

Paul started dancing again and very slowly inched his briefs down until his arse was uncovered and the base of his cock, he was blushing like a school boy and feeling very nervous as he took about three or four minutes to slide them off completely. He swung round revealing his cute arse and then back again to show a very tasty cock. Getting redder by the second he started to play with himself until he had a solid erection. It looked impressive, about seven or eight inches uncut and standing out at 45 degrees to his tummy. He stood with his hands behind his head, feet astride and swaying to the music. When the music stopped he dropped to his knees and covered himself as best he could.

"The most important part starts now. The music will change and you'll jump down from the stage and wander among the tables. When one of the ladies touches you stay where you are until she loses interest and then move on. Depending what they do to you will usually determine the size of the note they stick in your waist string. The only men in the club will be one of the owners and you strippers, plus security at the door, but you won't see them. If one of the ladies indicates she wants to play with your arse, and even finger you, you will let it happen without hesitating, the same with any playing at the front, including make you suck one another."

Four very determined looking guys stayed. The other gay one eased the tension and made everyone laugh.

"Oh yes, me first, I can eat Paul's cock and let him feed it all to me in one push, Darling."

Paul blushed almost scarlet but he jumped down from the table and walked towards the lady boss making all the comments. She started caressing his cock and balls, watching his face.

"Open your legs wide, Paul."

If you enjoyed this sample then look for **Take It Off.**

Andrew Todd

Riding High
Hot Gay Romance Erotica

The sharp rap on the door, followed by an urgent, "Zak, are you up!?" made Zak bolt upright in bed.

"'M up, Mom, I'm up," he mumbled.

"We have to leave in a half hour; you need to be downstairs in 15 minutes if you want to have breakfast before I drop you off at work."

"Ok, I'll be right down."

He heard her walk away from the door and head back downstairs. He lied back down on his bed, pulled his pillow over his face and screamed as loud as he could. Being awakened at 6:30 on a Saturday morning was not his idea of a great start to a weekend. When his mom had suggested he get a summer job, he had at first been excited. He was turning 19 and his mom had promised him he would inherit her old Toyota, but he would have to be able to pay for the insurance and gas.

He had gone right to the library and Mrs. Clinton the librarian was thrilled to offer him a job as an assistant librarian. He would mainly work in the kid's section helping younger kids with their summer reading and helping out in general in the library. He thought he was set for a nice, easy, air-conditioned summer. But, his mother had other plans. She had secured him a job at a local ranch. She insisted that he be outdoors during the summer, and that he be more active. His only physical activity during the school year was swimming at the YMCA two or three days a week. He was a great swimmer, but he was not interested in joining the team. Her insistence that he take this job had resulted in Zak basically giving his mom the silent treatment for the past week.

And what was worse, in order to get him 'ready' for his new job, he had to spend every Saturday and Sunday there for the last month of the school year. After school ended he would work there five or six days a week. He wasn't exactly sure what would be expected of him. He figured he'd be shoveling shit most of the summer. However, he figured if he screwed up enough this weekend, maybe they would fire him and he could get his library job back.

Looking at the clock he realized time was getting away from him. He jumped out of bed and ran to his bathroom. He turned on the shower and, after dropping his briefs on the floor jumped in. He quickly showered and then stepped out and started to towel himself off. He caught a glimpse of himself in the mirror. His blond hair was starting to get shaggy, but he had decided to let it grow out this summer. He didn't think he was the worst looking person in the world. In fact, he considered himself plain, but had heard some girls at school whispering about him. Apparently they thought more of his looks than he did. He had a slight swimmer's build, lean and taut. He was slender and short for his age, barely measuring 5' 4". He was hoping for a growth spurt this summer, but since his mom topped out at 5' 3" and his dad had been only about 5" 7' (at least according to his mom), he figured that ship had pretty much sailed.

He did not remember his dad, who had died in a car accident when he was only a toddler. His blond hair and blue eyes he got from his mom and according to her, he got his love of books and imagination from his dad. He would often look at the pictures of his dad and wonder what the last 15 years would have been like if it hadn't been just him and his mom.

After his dad passed, his mom had taken the BA in Accounting that she earned just prior to marrying his dad and parlayed it into a Vice Presidency at a local bank. She was a bit of a workaholic, but had been able to provide a nice home for Zak and her job offered them financial security and stability.

He stepped out of the bathroom and went to his dresser. He had no idea what he should wear, since he had little to no idea what his job would entail. He didn't want to wear anything that might be irrevocably ruined since he had the feeling there would be a lot of muck and dirt in his future. He figured he would go with some ratty old jeans and an old t-shirt. He also decided to wear his old sneakers since he wasn't about to run around a ranch in his new Chucks. It was only about 60 degrees out so he grabbed his old black hoodie and ran downstairs.

His mom was leaning against the counter drinking what was probably her third or fourth cup of coffee.

"Well, it's about time. I was about to go knock down your door."

"I'm ready." He looked out the kitchen window. "Mom, it's barely even light out. Are you sure I'm supposed to be there this early?"

"Yes, Jim said Mr. Jones was expecting you there at 7:30 this morning and that he would expect you to be there until 6 tonight and 4 tomorrow. He's not keeping you as long on Sundays right now because of school." Jim was a co-worker of his mom's; Mr. Jones, the owner of the ranch, was a friend of his and when Jim heard he was looking for summer help he told Zak's mom and the rest was settled before Zak knew what hit him.

"Did Jim know exactly what I would be doing?"

"Well, it's a horse ranch so I would imagine there will be a shovel in your future."

He shot his mom a dirty look as she grinned at him. "Ha, Ha," he rolled his eyes. "What makes you think this is the job for me? I've never even been to a ranch and the last time I was near a horse was the pony ride at the fair when I was five."

"Zak, Jim told Mr. Jones all about you, the work you do with younger kids at the library and the Y and about how good you are with computers; he also told him that you needed to get outdoors more."

"Mom..."

"Let me finish. I know you had your heart set on the library job, but you know as well as I do that this job will pay you a lot more than working at the town library. You'll be able to earn more, you'll be out in the fresh air, and maybe you'll make some new friends."

'Ah-ha', he thought, 'the other shoe has dropped.' His mom was always dancing around the fact that he was essentially a loner. He had a few friends at school, but they were just that: school friends. He spent most of his time alone or at the library or the Y where he mainly worked with kids that were younger than him. He was often uncomfortable and tongue-tied around people his own age. Most people at school saw him as a small, smart, shy nerd and he didn't disagree with their opinion of him.

He had known he was 'different' since he was much younger and it wasn't until puberty hit that he was able to put his finger on what made him different than the other boys at school. While they were chasing the girls, all Zak could think about was chasing them. He had never seen what his male classmates saw in their female counterparts. But just being in the boys' locker room made his heart race. He knew that if anyone of his classmates knew his secret, his life would be unlivable. They might spend a lot of time in the media telling you 'It Gets Better', but you had to survive 'It' first.

From the moment the realization of his sexuality hit him, he had found himself more comfortable with younger kids. They were honest and he had fun teaching little kids to swim and read and helping them with schoolwork. When he was working with the little kids, he didn't have to worry about being turned on or aroused. He could relax, and in those moments he could be himself, not the guarded automaton he was in school.

His mom's voice woke him from his daydream. "Well, we need to get going."

"Ok, I'm ready." He grabbed a banana off the counter and ran to the fridge to grab a bottle of juice.

They didn't talk much on the way to ranch. Zak's mom knew he was nervous about this job and she felt a little guilty about forcing him to take it, but she was concerned about him. He spent too much time indoors and with kids much younger than he was. She knew he had a brilliant future as a teacher or in some other career working with kids, but she felt he needed to get outside and make some friends his own age. She didn't know if the friends part would be accomplished with this job, but she was glad he wouldn't be spending the summer all cooped up inside. Making the deal to give him her old car was worth it to make him accept this job.

The ranch was about 15 miles outside of town. Zak was again daydreaming as they drove. He was nervous, but he knew his mom was right about the money thing. His library job would have been one step above a volunteer role. They might have been able to pay him a few dollars a day and some of the parents would pay him to tutor, but the ranch job was paying him $10 an hour. The kids working at the local fast food joints weren't going to make that much. He'd promised his mom that he would try his best and he would, knowing that if he screwed up he could still get the library job back. Mrs. Clinton had made it clear that she was creating the job for him and she would not be filling just for the sake of filling it.

He looked up to see that his mom was turning down a dirt road. Ahead of them was a large locked gate. Over the gate was a sign reading 'Triple J Ranch'. The car came to a stop.

"OK, Sweetie, I'm going to drop you here so I can get to work. Mr. Jones said to just go through the gate and go straight up the road and he would meet you at the barn. Do you have your phone, so you can call if you need anything?"

"I've got it, but I should be ok."

She leaned over to give him a quick kiss on the cheek. "I know you will. Just do your best and try to have fun, maybe you'll end up liking it."

He looked at her as if she had just taken complete leave of her senses. "I'll try, Mom."

"I'll be back to pick you up at 6."

He started to get out of the car.

"I love you, Zak."

"Love you, too, Mom."

He watched as his mom turned the car around and went back down the dirt road.

He walked over and unlatched the fence. He walked through the gate and locked it behind him. He might not know anything about a ranch, but he didn't want to get blamed for any animals getting out of the gate.

He looked up and saw nothing but woods and a long dirt road. He started walking down the road. He had walked for about 10 minutes when he finally saw a large building he assumed was the barn. He walked towards the building. When he was about 500 feet from the entrance of the building, he saw a huge dog come running out of the building and straight towards him. The dog was barking loudly and coming right at him. Zak stopped in his tracks thinking that he was going to be this dog's breakfast before he even started his job.

The dog came at him full speed and jumped up on him hitting him square in the chest with its front paws. The dog caught him off guard and Zak fell backwards and landed on his butt. He closed his eyes and waited for the jaws of this beast to go for his throat. When nothing happened he slowly opened one eye; the dog was standing over him and Zak could swear it was grinning at him. It took a step forward and licked him straight up his face from chin to forehead. Zak couldn't help himself, he sat there and started laughing while the dog continued to bathe his face.

"Ember!!" He looked up and saw a man marching out of the barn towards them. "Get off that poor boy!!"

The man stopped in front of them and the dog stopped licking Zak's face and walked over to the man. He reached down to offer Zak a hand up. "You must be Zachary."

Zak jumped to his feet and brushed himself off. 'Yes, sir, Zachary Myers, but most people just call me Zak."

"Nice to meet you, Zak, I'm Martin Jones and you've met Ember. Sorry about her greeting you that way. She's too damn friendly to be much of a watchdog. She's more likely to lick a trespasser to death."

"Oh, that's ok. She just startled me. I haven't been around animals too much. What kind of dog is she?"

"She's a Golden Retriever. They're known for being a big friendly ball of fluff and this one is that in spades. As much as I wish she was a little more of a protector, given the number of people we have come and go at the ranch, I guess I'm lucky she's as friendly as she is."

Sensing she was no longer in trouble, Ember walked over to Zak and moved her head under his hand. Zak smiled down at the dog and scratched her head.

"Well, I see she's made another friend," Mr. Jones laughed. "Why don't you come with me into the barn so we can talk some?"

Zak slowly followed Mr. Jones into the barn. Ember stayed right with him; given his small stature he was able to keep petting her while they walked.

Mr. Jones led him into a small office area. He sat in a chair behind the desk and motioned for Zak to have a seat across from him. Zak sat down and Ember sat in attention right next to him.

"Son, are you sure you don't have a dog at home?"

"No, sir, I asked my mom for one when I was little, but she thought it would be too much for me at the time and I never thought about it since, why?"

"Well, she's usually friendly and rambunctious, but I've never seen her take to someone as quickly as she's taken to you. The only other person she follows around like that is one of my other hands, but that guy has a way with animals that I've never seen in another person. Maybe we'll find out you have that same gift."

Before Zak could stop himself, he laughed out loud. Mr. Jones looked at him curiously.

"I'm sorry, Mr. Jones, I don't mean to be rude, but I have never been around animals at all. My mom sprang this job on me as a surprise. I promised her that I would do my best and give it a try, but I've never been an outdoor person or an animal person. I like animals, but I've never had any experience with them."

"Zak, I appreciate your candor. I'll be just as honest with you. When my friend Jim asked me about taking you on, I was a little apprehensive, but he spoke of you glowingly. He told me you were a smart, courteous young man who spent a great deal of his time teaching and helping others. That's what I'm looking for this summer. Yes, there will be lots of hard work and manual labor, but we have a lot of fun here as well. We're not a huge operation. It's basically me and two hands and now you. We have about 20 horses, give or take. Most are owned by me, but we do have a few boarders. We give lessons and offer trail rides. I know horses can be intimidating for some people, and you might feel a little nervous around them at first, especially given your smaller stature, but my first advice for you is to remember to let them know who is boss. I've seen a 17-hand horse follow a small child around the ring, cuz the kid let that horse know he was in charge."

"You have a horse with 17 hands?"

Mr. Jones let out a loud belly laugh. "Sorry, you're going to have a lot of horse lingo thrown at you over the next couple days. Hands are the way you measure a horse. One hand is roughly 4 inches and you measure them to the top of their withers--that's their shoulder."

"So that's a big horse?"

"Yes, very big. Most of ours are between 14 ½ and 16 hands. And most of them are extremely gentle and friendly. They have to be; if I can't trust them with inexperienced riders, I'd lose my business."

"So, what exactly will I be doing?"

"Well, for the next few weekends, I'm going to turn you over to one of my hands, Dusty. He'll go over what we expect from you and walk you through everything. The only thing I ask is that you listen carefully to everything he tells you and if anything doesn't make sense or you're not quite sure, always ask."

"Yes, sir, I will," Zak replied, thinking to himself, 'Oh, great I'm gonna spend the weekend with some old cowboy with a cliché for a name.'

As he rose from his chair, Mr. Jones said, "Dusty should be here any minute and then I'll turn you over to him. I think you'll like it here, Zak."

He offered his hand to Zak and Zak shook it.

"Thank you, Mr. Jones, I'll try my best."

"I believe you will, son. Now, I need to check on some things in the other barn. Why don't you wait here; like I said, Dusty should be here any minute. I'm sure your new girlfriend will be more than happy to keep you company."

Zak laughed as Mr. Jones left the office. He leaned over in his chair and rubbed the big dog's ears and petted her sides. He had been honest with Mr. Jones; after the one time he asked his mom for a dog, he had never thought about it again. His mom had given him a lot to try to make up for his dad not being there, but she never tried to spoil him. Even at five, he had known she was right; neither of them was in a place to take care of a dog and since he did not have many friends, he had no experience with animals at their houses either. Looking down at Ember, he suddenly thought that maybe if things went well he might ask his mom if he could get a dog now. She knew he was responsible and she always wanted him outside and a dog would get him out for walks. That was something to think about.

He sat in the office for about 10 minutes just petting and talking to the dog; he was starting to feel more relaxed and thinking that maybe this wouldn't be the train wreck he was anticipating.

He heard someone come into the barn and assumed it was Mr. Jones. Ember's ears pricked up and she took off like a shot out of the office.

"Hey, Emmy, how are you?" he heard a voice saying. It wasn't Mr. Jones.

As he was getting out of his chair to investigate, Ember came charging back into the office followed by the most beautiful boy he had ever seen. He was about 18, deeply tanned, with black eyes and long black hair pulled back in a ponytail. He was wearing faded jeans, scuffed-up leather boots, a wife beater and a denim jacket. He had to be almost 6 feet tall and was slim and muscular.

Zak just stared as the other boy offered his hand.

"Hey, you must be Zak," he said with a radiant smile. "I'm Dusty."

Zak stood up and took the offered hand and shook it.

"Oh, man," he thought. "It's going to be a long summer."

If you enjoyed this sample then look for **Riding High.**

Gay Romance Erotica
MASTERED
SENSUAL TALES FROM ANCIENT EGYPT
DEXTER CHASE

The Egyptians were rampant, raiding across the middle sea, raping and pillaging, but worst of all taking many slaves.It was always the youngest and most nubile of females and the prepubescent and middle teen boys. Those chosen were taken as sex slaves, to be used for their masters own sexual satisfaction and at times to be shared by other masters and forced to take part in orgies. The orgies that would make the later Roman ones pale into insignificance. I knew about the Roman orgies because that Empire grew as I too grew up, and I would eventually be taken there as an overseer for all the younger slaves that were taken from Egypt. Slaves in Egypt were invariably naked and most of the large houses had a bevy of young male and female slaves kept almost entirely for sex.

It was into one of these great houses that I was taken after being captured in one of the raids. I, too became one of those slaves all those years ago. I had passed into puberty and grown into a quite imposing youth at eighteen at the time I was captured. My new master was probably no older than thirty five but already he had a son my own age and several younger ones. He was a high ranking soldier and as one would expect he had a magnificent body. Before I became a slave, I had been mentored by a friend of my father's after puberty so I was well practiced in the art of man to man sex, us Greeks were not at all conscious that men having sex with boys was anything abnormal. The Egyptians didn't think like that so I was quite surprised that my master would fuck me frequently but I noticed he never allowed other men to fuck his eldest son. The eldest son was called Ptolemy, at eighteen he was almost too pretty to be a boy, made more so by the makeup he used on his eyes. I think I started to fall in love with him from the first day I saw him. He was always beautifully dressed and wandered around the villa with seemingly nothing to do. He would watch me work sometimes when his father was away and as I started to learn his language, he started talking to me.

By the time I was twenty his father had rather lost interest in me so I was trained to look after Ptolomy, his clothes all had to be perfect and ready to use at any time. The first time I left some of his clothes out instead of carefully putting them away I found that he was very strong and could be quite wicked.

"Ajax, how dare you leave my clothes like this?"

I realised he was very angry and fell to my knees begging his forgiveness.

"Of course I'm going to forgive you, after I have punished you. Come."

I knew where we were going. I had been to the punishment room before whenever I had displeased my master. I resigned myself to receiving a huge tranche of pain as I was whipped and knew that I would probably be in bed for a week unable to recline on my back. I was surprised at what happened, it was the first time that I had not been permanently marked. The slave master must have been an expert. A huge amount of debilitating pain but the skin hadn't been broked so I was not scarred.

"You have to learn that my clothes must always be perfect Ajax. What do you think would be an appropriate punishment for your dereliction of duty?"

He was being very imperious, but his manner made him appear very sexy and my wayward cock showed my arousal very quickly. It was very hard by the time Ptolomy had finished talking to me. The look on his face made me realise he had not seen my penis erect before. I didn't consider it to be huge, but it was certainly quite impressive. The master had enjoyed playing with it sometimes, but mostly he would just take me on his couch and fuck me quickly for mere satisfaction, he never made love to me. I think he found it easier to have the sex he wanted without all the complications of pregnancy and when he wanted to make love, he would take his wife. So different to my life in Athens. My mentor showed me how joyous lovemaking between males could be, my father had picked well and I knew when my time came I would make my wife happy and mentor the son of a friend when I was older. At that moment , I had no idea what would happen to me. I supposed that if I was less comely I would be sent to one of the work gangs building the pyramid to house the next pharaoh to die and I would be worked to death.

If you enjoyed this sample then look for **Mastered**.

Son Swap

ANGUS MACGREGOR

HOT GAY EROTICA

Walking over the top of the ridge, Paul Gibson smiled as the blue vista of the Pacific Ocean greeted his eyes. Sam came up behind him and laid a heavy hand on his shoulder. Both men were panting. The last hundred yards of the hiking trail had been practically vertical, but it paid off in a spectacular fashion. The view stretched from Seaside all the way south to Tillamook. The canopy of Douglas fir and Sitka spruce had opened up to reveal a turquoise sky that blended in with the vast azure of the ocean far below.

"Okay," Sam panted. "You were right, buddy. This was definitely worth the five miles. Holy shit! It's so beautiful."

"I know. When Cole and I came up here last spring, I was pretty blown away so I definitely wanted you to see it."

The men stood on the edge of the cliff. The wind blew their hair and thin hiking shorts around like sails. The air was cool to their sweaty chests, bare and beaded with sweat. It was a hot day for the north Oregon coast. They had passed only one other hiker on the trail and he was headed back down to the trail head. Paul took a long drink of water and passed the bottle to Sam who finished it. Paul took another step closer to the edge of the cliff and pulled out his dick and sent a long golden stream over the rim toward the crashing surf far surging beneath.

"Look out below," he bellowed laughing. Sam pulled out his dick and joined the party, two yellow arcs glistening in the sunlight.

"This is one of those moments when I just couldn't imagine being a woman. I love pissing outside so easy like this."

"I'm with you, buddy. Add that to my list of gratitude for being a dude. I'm sure there's plenty of wonderful things about being a girl, but since I really don't get it, I'm happy to be pissing into the wind with you right now," Sam said with a chuckle. "Damn, this cool breeze is giving me a chub."

"You always have a chub, buddy," Paul said, shaking his penis but leaving it hanging out of his shorts. "Maybe we should do the hike back naked? You brave enough?"

"Sure. We've ran into naked hikers before. No one ever says anything. It's Oregon for God's sake."

"So true."

"We should bring our boys up here and see if they would go for a naked hike. Would be fun to see them out here like that. You want some jerky?" Paul dug a baggie full of beef jerky from his backpack and passed some to Sam. It was sweet and spicy. The men chewed the beef and continued to point to landmarks and enjoy the brilliance of the perfect afternoon.

"So often when you get out here, it fogs up and you can hardly see anything. This day is amazing," Sam said with a mouth full of jerky. "You gonna stand there all day with your dick hanging out?"

"Yeah, I might. You sure seem to like staring at my Johnson."

Sam laughed. "You and I have been staring at one another for quite a while now. You'd think we'd be used to it. But I still enjoy the view whenever I get a chance."

Paul pulled the man toward him in a close embrace. Sam's skin felt warm and soft against his own. Sam's dark furry belly pressed close against his smooth one. Their faces were close, lips and noses only separated by a tiny space. Paul reached up and touched Sam's jaw. The dark stubble was prickly to his fingers but for some reason, this made his penis swell. Sam's rough hand gripped his shaft and ran his thumb across the piss slit, now slick with precum. Paul's hand slid inside Sam's shorts and gripped the man's thick, solid cock. The full bush felt soft and ticklish to his hand. He slid his hand around the man's sack and let the plum sized testicles roll in his palm. His breath increased and he closed his eyes as Sam's soft, thick lips brushed against his.

"Man, this never gets old, my friend," Sam whispered against his lips.

"I know, bro. It just keeps getting better…"

If you enjoyed this sample then look for **Son Swap**.